LITTLE WHITE LIES

I wondered if Scott had told his friends he'd asked me out. I studied them carefully and listened to their conversation. I felt pretty left out, until Scott started talking about hockey.

I seized the opportunity and told him that Rory O'Toole, the hockey star, had been over at my house to see my father. Scott's eyes widened at that. I didn't explain that Rory called me the Muppet, meaning I was cute but not to be taken seriously. Or that Rory was only interested in his glorious reflection in our hall mirror. No, I couldn't reveal the truth to Scott. He clearly worshiped Rory O'Toole.

Instead, I said, "Wait until I tell Rory I'm friends with Scott Holbrook. He'll be impressed." Actually, he'd probably ask me who Scott was. But it was only a little white lie, and it brought the widest grin to Scott's gorgeous face. Who could it hurt?

Bantam Sweet Dreams Romances
Ask your bookseller for the books you have missed

P.S. I LOVE YOU by Barbara Conklin
THE POPULARITY PLAN by Rosemary Vernon
LAURIE'S SONG by Suzanne Rand
PRINCESS AMY by Melinda Pollowitz
LITTLE SISTER by Yvonne Greene
CALIFORNIA GIRL by Janet Quin-Harkin
GREEN EYES by Suzanne Rand
THE THOROUGHBRED by Joanna Campbell
COVER GIRL by Yvonne Greene
LOVE MATCH by Janet Quin-Harkin
THE PROBLEM WITH LOVE by Rosemary Vernon
NIGHT OF THE PROM by Debra Spector
THE SUMMER JENNY FELL IN LOVE by Barbara Conklin
DANCE OF LOVE by Jocelyn Saal
THINKING OF YOU by Jeanette Nobile
HOW DO YOU SAY GOODBYE by Margaret Burman
ASK ANNIE by Suzanne Rand
TEN-BOY SUMMER by Janet Quin-Harkin
LOVE SONG by Anne Park
THE POPULARITY SUMMER by Rosemary Vernon
ALL'S FAIR IN LOVE by Jeanne Andrews
SECRET IDENTITY by Joanna Campbell
FALLING IN LOVE AGAIN by Barbara Conklin
THE TROUBLE WITH CHARLIE by Jaye Ellen
HER SECRET SELF by Rhondi Vilott
IT MUST BE MAGIC by Marian Woodruff
TOO YOUNG FOR LOVE by Gailanne Maravel
TRUSTING HEARTS by Jocelyn Saal
NEVER LOVE A COWBOY by Jesse DuKore
LITTLE WHITE LIES by Lois I. Fisher
TOO CLOSE FOR COMFORT by Debra Spector
DAYDREAMER by Janet Quin-Harkin
DEAR AMANDA by Rosemary Vernon
COUNTRY GIRL by Melinda Pollowitz
FORBIDDEN LOVE by Marian Woodruff
SUMMER DREAMS by Barbara Conklin
PORTRAIT OF LOVE by Jeanette Nobile
RUNNING MATES by Jocelyn Saal
FIRST LOVE by Debra Spector
SECRETS by Anna Aaron
THE TRUTH ABOUT ME & BOBBY V. by Janetta Johns
THE PERFECT MATCH by Marian Woodruff
TENDER LOVING CARE by Anne Park
LONG DISTANCE LOVE by Jesse DuKore
DREAM PROM by Margaret Burman
ON THIN ICE by Jocelyn Saal
TE AMO MEANS I LOVE YOU by Deborah Kent
DIAL L FOR LOVE by Marian Woodruff
TOO MUCH TO LOSE by Suzanne Rand
LIGHTS, CAMERA, LOVE by Gailanne Maravel
MAGIC MOMENTS by Debra Spector
LOVE NOTES by Joanna Campbell
GHOST OF A CHANCE by Janet Quin-Harkin
I CAN'T FORGET YOU by Lois I. Fisher
SPOTLIGHT ON LOVE by Nancy Pines
CAMPFIRE NIGHTS by Dale Cowan

Little White Lies

Lois I. Fisher

BANTAM BOOKS
TORONTO · NEW YORK · LONDON · SYDNEY

RL 4, IL age 11 and up

LITTLE WHITE LIES
A Bantam Book / January 1983

2nd printing . . . January 1983
3rd printing . . . June 1983
4th printing . . . February 1984

Cover photo by Pat Hill

ISBN 0-553-24293-8

Published simultaneously in the United States and Canada

Bantam Books are published by Bantam Books, Inc. Its trademark, consisting of the words "Bantam Books" and the portrayal of a rooster, is Registered in U.S. Patent and Trademark Office and in other countries. Marca Registrada. Bantam Books, Inc., 666 Fifth Avenue, New York, New York 10103.

PRINTED IN THE UNITED STATES OF AMERICA

O 13 12 11 10 9 8 7 6 5 4

Little White Lies

Chapter One

Had I actually volunteered to be the first speaker in oral communications class? What a mistake! At the start of the period, Ms. Perez, who was young and bouncy, had asked for a volunteer, and I had foolishly raised my hand. Then she began talking, and I thought she had forgotten about it. I began hoping I wouldn't have to give the speech until the next day.

Wrong. About three-quarters of the way through the period, she called on me. All eyes turned my way. My heart was pounding out a drum roll. All those eyes, except Audrey Van's, were new to me. My sophomore schedule in immense, crowded Lincoln High had neatly sidestepped the schedules of my old friends from Maitland Junior High. Instead, it coincided with those of the kids from Dalton Junior High. And everybody knew about *them*.

The kids from "the shore." They were elite, a sophisticated clique, sought after. A tight little group that didn't take to newcomers, especially if they were not from the Jersey shore. And the way they dressed! Take Daisy Clements, who had favored me with a haughty glance when Ms. Perez announced I'd be the guinea pig. Daisy was put together like an ad for Talbot's.

You probably think I'm quiet and shy. Say that to my old friends from Maitland and they'd laugh you all the way from New Jersey to New York City. "Nina Ward? You've got to be kidding!" My relatives, especially my uncle Timothy and aunt Zelda from New York City, would roar. See, I have this talent for storytelling. I like being in the limelight. I'm called the Official Ward Family tale-spinner.

"I've never seen anyone with such a flair for telling tales," my uncle is fond of saying. "Only you could convince my twins that the tooth fairy gives out loot when a tooth comes in as well as when one comes out."

Uncle Timothy has promised me a job with his Madison Avenue advertising firm when I graduate from college.

My closest friend, Peggy Blair—who doesn't share *one* class with me, can you believe that? —used to hold ghost-story contests when I'd sleep over at her house. The one who told the scariest story got treated to a double sundae at Swensen's. I got taken there so often I have the entire flavor list committed to memory.

But making up stories for Uncle Timothy's two sets of twins and for Peggy was entirely different from getting up in front of a class full of strangers and delivering a three-minute speech, minus notes, on "My Most Exciting Day of the Summer."

All I could think about were the Dalton kids. In addition to Daisy, there was Ace Turner, the acknowledged funny man. He was tall, thin, with the grace of a ballet dancer. His reddish hair gleamed, and his blue eyes sparkled with mischief. He exclusively dated Ginger Callison, also in the class, and clearly the female leader of the Daltonites. She was also tall and thin, with shoulder-length, burnished copper hair and the biggest blue eyes in the world. When she walked with Ace, they looked like a matched set of designer luggage. Her locker was next to mine, and she always said hello. At least she was friendly, which was more than you could say about most Daltonites.

Other Daltonites included the incredibly sexy Scott Holbrook.

"Nina!"

From the way Ms. Perez's voice lifted and from the snickers of the kids, I gathered she'd called my name more than once. I stood shakily and prayed that I would make it from my seat to the front of the class without tripping over anything. I was thankful I'd chosen my new kilt and red-trimmed navy pullover to wear, for basically I do not look terrific. My wavy, blond hair is washed out, the strands thin; my green eyes are small and sparkleless; and I'm short. My complexion is clear at least. One out of four. Oh, well.

I reached the front. Why did the room look bigger from that vantage point? Why couldn't I know someone other than Audrey Van? We were never really friends back at Maitland. Oh, well, at least, she was a familiar face. I'd concentrate on her when I spoke.

"Ok, begin, Nina," said Ms. Perez. "Three minutes."

Or one hundred and eighty grueling seconds.

I opened my dry mouth. "My most exciting day of the summer was the day I took the Bobbsey twins to Yankee Stadium." No recognition in Audrey's wide face. Well, all she ever read was *Vogue*. Were the other kids as unaware, too? From the dead air, I supposed they were.

"The Bobbsey twins are my cousins. I call

them that because of the books I read when I was a kid. Two pairs of twins, ages five and seven." A loud yawn from the vicinity of Daisy Clements. I closed my mouth and bit down on my lip. The speech had been rehearsed in front of my mirror and my mother, who said I told a pleasant story. Pleasant obviously didn't count with the Daltonites.

"Everything was fine with taking them to Yankee Stadium until we boarded the subway. Then I wondered: a, if I had lost my mind; b, if I should give up baby-sitting for something a little easier, like driving in demolition derbies; c, why anyone would want to have children; or d, all of the above."

Bits of laughter. Not snickers, real chuckles. Audrey wasn't a laugher. I decided to focus on someone else. Ginger Callison sat in the second row, third seat. She was smiling. I looked directly at her.

"First off, we were in the first car, and the little twins wanted to stand in the front and look out the window while the big twins walked through the car, reading all the graffiti and demanding to know what certain words meant—in very loud voices. Also, the car was jammed with Salvation Army people."

By now, everybody was laughing in the appropriate places. I decided my original speech would have to be embroidered upon. I added to it as I went along. The foul ball I'd caught off a bench player for the Baltimore Orioles became a homer off the bat of Dave Winfield. The slight delay in getting home via the subway turned into a derailment.

When I finished, applause broke out. My neck reddened. Ms. Perez, who was holding a stopwatch, said, "Very entertaining, Nina, but you ran forty seconds over."

"Who cares?" Ace called out. "It was great!"

"Yeah!" Ginger seconded.

"It was pretty good," Daisy said.

"I admit Nina will be a hard act to follow, but remember, when I say three minutes, I mean three minutes."

I rushed back to my desk, narrowly missing a book bag in the aisle.

"Sorry, it shouldn't be there."

I knew the voice belonged to Scott Holbrook, but I couldn't look at him. Just the fact that he'd spoken to me made my heart zigzag through my chest.

The bell rang. I gathered up my books and headed for the back door. Several kids stopped to compliment me. I smiled and nodded my thanks, too dumbfounded to speak. When I reached the door, I walked smack into Scott Holbrook.

Scott was the male leader of the Daltonites. He was close to six feet, husky, with thick, dark hair, deep gray eyes edged with lashes anyone would like to have, and a smile that lit up his eyes like the Christmas tree in Rockefeller Center.

"That was a great speech," he said. "I can tell you really like baseball. Do you like other sports?"

I was terribly aware of the rest of his crowd waiting for him in the hall. Oral communications was a seventh-period class, the end of the day for many sophomores, including me.

"Oh, yeah," I said enthusiastically. "I like hockey, too." Scott beamed. Of course, he had to know I knew he was a member of the Roadrunners, the Lincoln hockey team, even if he hadn't played a game for them yet. In junior high Scott had a super reputation. When Dalton played Maitland's motley rejects—we went zero and fourteen last season—he scored a hat trick.

"My father is a professor at Parkhurst," I said quietly. "Rory O'Toole, the captain of the Spitfires, is in his English class."

Scott's gorgeous eyes widened. Rory amounted to a legend. The NHL had its eyes on him. They could have him, too. Rory

O'Toole was the most conceited, pompous bore at Parkhurst College.

"That's really something. Listen, you have lunch fourth period, right? I've seen you in the cafeteria. Come by our table tomorrow, OK?"

"OK." I nearly fainted.

He and the other Daltonites formed a pack and descended a nearby staircase. I slumped against the wall. Most of the kids from Maitland had lunch fifth period. I'd been eating alone or sometimes with Audrey Van, which was kind of like eating alone because we weren't on the same wavelength. We had different interests. Audrey was about twenty pounds overweight, which didn't faze her a bit because she got lots of work as a chubby model. However, I didn't think all that excess baggage was healthy. And naturally, since I'd known Audrey forever, I wasn't afraid to speak my mind to her. She did not appreciate my comments. So when we ate together, we mostly discussed algebra, a subject we both agreed could go the way of Latin. We did not have a whole lot of fun together. Lunch with anyone else would have been a huge treat.

Because I'm from Maitland, which is where Lincoln High is located, I didn't take a bus home. Instead, I walked—well, more like floated—the seven blocks to my tree-lined street. Scott Holbrook wanted me to eat lunch with him! I could hardly wait to tell Peggy. She would absolutely turn somersaults. But I'd have to wait until after the eighth period when her classes were over, or maybe even later if she had a date with Jack, her steady boyfriend. Wouldn't it be fabulous to have a *real* boyfriend? I thought. Someone like Scott? *Slow down*, I told myself. *He's only asked you to join his group for lunch.*

Sighing, I entered the house. My father was home. The smell of his pipe came from his den.

"Hello, Dad!" I stuck my head into the smoke-filled room.

He quickly snuffed the pipe. He'd given up cigarettes last year and gone the pipe route. Mom and I didn't agree with him that a pipe was OK to smoke. In fact, we hated it, since it tended to pollute the entire house. Dad, who's very gentle and understanding, agreed not to smoke when Mom or I was in the house.

"And I just lit up." He sighed. "How are you, Nina? You look a bit flushed."

"I'm surprised you can see me through the smoke haze." We laughed. I couldn't tell him about Scott. Dad's a good father, but he thinks I still play Candyland. I merely said, "I gave my speech today. In fact, I volunteered. Your daughter can do very strange things sometimes."

"Since you're not in a thousand pieces, I assume the speech went according to plan?"

"Mmm, you might say that." Before he could ask what that cryptic remark meant, I added, "I think I got an A-minus. I ran forty seconds over the limit."

"With the way you talk, I'm not surprised. Listen, if you want a delicious snack, try the coconut cookies I baked this morning before my first class." Dad had a light schedule on Tuesdays.

When he gave up smoking, he took up baking. Since Mom and the oven don't get along, it has worked out beautifully. After consuming five cookies and a Coke, I went up to my room to call Peggy, hoping she was home. She was!

"I'm glad you called," she said. "I never see you anymore. Not even in the halls!"

"You don't see anything with Jack draped around you," I reminded her. I cleared my throat. "I just may go that route soon, too."

"You may have Jack draped around you? I'd better have a talk with him."

We giggled, then I said, "I didn't exactly have Jack Adams in mind. More like Scott Holbrook."

She dropped the phone. The crash echoed in my ear. "You mean *the* Scott Holbrook?" she asked after she picked up the receiver. "Of the *Dalton* group?"

Peggy made "the Dalton group" sound like a rock band that had caused an international scandal. I knew they weren't her favorites. "Too much flash, no substance," she said when she first saw them climb off the bus. "It comes from living on the shore."

I have never said anything, but I think Peggy's jealous. Her parents once owned a successful business, but then Mr. Blair got sick and the business went bankrupt, leaving the Blairs with only the roof over their heads. The Daltonites were wealthy, and they weren't secretive about the fact.

I quickly told her about the speech and what Scott had said. I ended with, "Eating with them would be a lot more exciting than staying with Audrey. Remember, you're surrounded by Maitland kids and Jack during your lunch."

"I'm sorry, Nina. I didn't mean to sound so negative. It's just that those kids are so—so—you know!"

"What?" I demanded. "Scott is friendly, and Ginger Callison has the locker next to mine. She always says hello."

"But what about her boyfriend? That noisy Ace Turner? And Daisy Clements—she's in my gym class, and her idea of working out is to brush her hair."

"Are you trying to tell me I won't fit in with them?"

She sensed the resentment in my voice, and immediately she said, "I'm sorry, Nina. It's just that they're so different. I wanted your first real boyfriend to be someone more like—like Jack or one of the kids from Maitland."

"I know what you mean," I admitted. "Scott Holbrook wasn't exactly what I expected, either. But aren't we jumping the gun a bit? I mean, he just asked me over to his table in the cafeteria, not to go out with him or anything."

Didn't I, somewhere inside, though, wish that would happen? I knew I wasn't being totally honest with Peggy. For my first *real* boyfriend I had envisioned someone *exactly* like Scott Holbrook. Handsome and debonair. Someone others would notice. Someone who would make other people say, "There go Scott and Nina. Aren't they a great couple?"

That was the kind of thing people said when they saw Ace and Ginger together. I wanted that. I *needed* that. But Peggy, with serious, poker-faced Jack, wouldn't understand that need.

However, she had brought up a point that nagged me as I fixed the tuna casserole and spinach salad for supper: the rest of the Daltonites. They came in a package. Scott had asked me over to *their* table: Ace with his witty remarks; Ginger with her glamour; Daisy with her sarcastic remarks; and the others. True, they'd enjoyed my speech, but would they enjoy me? Would I be cool enough for their group?

Chapter Two

My mother was positive the group would adore me, just the way Scott seemed to. She's pretty terrific for someone who's forty-two.

"You'll get along fine," she said after dinner while we filled the dishwasher. "He's a hockey player. You love hockey. The others probably like it, too. That's your first common denominator. I'm sure you'll discover more."

"I'm not."

Mom has no trouble talking to *anyone.* Why not? She's a librarian, and librarians are a warehouse of information. "What were the names of the pandas China gave to Nixon?" Snap! She knows the answer. "What was the title of Stephen King's first horror novel?" Wham! She knows that, too.

I possess no such fund of knowledge. True, my imagination is plentiful. But that wouldn't help me. Or would it? My creative imagination added to my speech, but that was in class. This would be real life.

Mom pushed a wisp of grayish blond hair off her forehead. "Nina, just go over to the table tomorrow. This boy wants you there. Forget about his friends."

But I couldn't do that! The Daltonites were just too tight. All for one and one for all. The Maitland kids weren't that way. Maybe because there were more of us. Dalton Junior High was small and exclusive, almost like a private school.

I dressed carefully that day, wishing I hadn't worn my kilt the day before. I looked through my closet four times and my dresser twice. Nothing looked right.

When I finally pulled a couple of things together, I glanced into the full-length mirror behind my bedroom door and sank onto the bed. I looked ordinary. If only my hair was thicker or my eyelashes darker. Mascara! I hunted through my tiny makeup bag. I applied one coat. Mom didn't approve of my wearing much makeup to school. She said she wanted my face to breathe.

I dashed out the door and gratefully caught up with Peggy and Jack, glad to be in the company of the kids I felt comfortable with. We laughed and joked and remembered the time in eighth grade when Chuck Vanci threw the first boy-girl party any of us had attended. We hadn't been sure what was supposed to happen at one, but afterward we rated it between a trip to the orthodontist and the sinking of the *Titanic*.

By the time we reached school, I felt much more relaxed.

The relaxed feeling did not last until lunchtime, however.

When I entered the cafeteria, my facial pores were the only parts of me breathing. There *they* were, at the long table in the middle of the lunchroom, laughing and having a great time. Scott wasn't with them. I sucked in my breath, took a giant step toward them, then a giant step away from them and toward the lunch line. I was paying for a strawberry yogurt and grapefruit juice when I felt a tap on my shoulder.

I glanced up into the unbelievably handsome face of Scott Holbrook. "I'm a little late," he said. "I had to talk with my guidance counselor. Are you all set?" He nodded to the tray.

"Sure. I was just waiting until you came along." *And if you'd forgotten, I would've died.*

Scott paid for his food. Then he picked up his tray in one hand, and with the other, he took my arm. The strength of his grip made me go all wobbly in the knees. We walked over to the Dalton table. They all looked up at me. Scott announced, "This is Nina. You know—oral communications?"

Mostly nods, a flurry of hellos, and quick smiles. While Scott brought over a chair from another table, Ginger said, "I like your sweater."

"Thanks!" At least I looked OK. If Ginger approved, the rest wouldn't disapprove. Not vocally, anyhow. I noticed Daisy Clements giving me the critical once-over. She didn't say anything.

I managed to sit down with some amount of grace. Marty Carmichael, also in oral communications, had center stage. "That party was too much! My folks had to hire a cleaning service to get the patio back into recognizable condition."

Marty Carmichael's parents owned a huge chain of supermarkets in Monmouth and Middlesex counties. They also owned a gorgeous house that had once appeared in the architecture section of *The New York Times Magazine*. Imagine going to a party there! It was right on the water.

"Do you surf?" Scott asked suddenly.

"Oh, no. I mean I've never tried. I like to

swim, though." Scott was a magnificent athlete. He probably rode the highest waves.

"That's great. I do both. But I'm just learning how to surf. I'm not very good yet. How are you on skates?"

"Not bad. I like to ice-skate." I would've added something about skating in Rockefeller Center with the twins, but he probably wouldn't have cared about mundane stuff like that.

The talk switched around rapidly from Ace's new car—he was a junior, the oldest of the group—to Daisy's plans for redecorating her bedroom in stark black and white. "Much more sophisticated than the dull baby blue and yellow I have now." I gulped, picturing my own yellow bedroom.

Ginger remarked that her brothers were clearing out their family's gazebo. A gazebo! I thought only heroines in Gothic novels had gazebos! I nearly asked her about it, but Mr. O'Leary, the football coach, strode through the cafeteria, and Marty called him over. I'd never have had the nerve to be so friendly with a teacher. But Mr. O'Leary didn't seem to mind. Marty was a defensive back. When the coach departed, the talk jumped to hockey, and everyone assured Scott he'd definitely be the first sophomore in Lincoln High history to be appointed team captain.

The conversation turned back to Marty's fabulous party, which had marked the end of summer freedom for the group. I also heard something about a birthday party for Wendie Wheeler, Marty's girl. "Poor thing is stuck with fifth-period lunch and those creepy, nowhere kids," Daisy said.

"But Wendie's a really nice person. She gets along with anybody," said Ginger. "I'm sure she has lots of friends during fifth period by now."

Daisy pouted. "I suppose so. She is my oldest friend, though, and I miss her terribly!"

Probably just the way I missed Peggy. But I couldn't say that to Daisy. I had the feeling Daisy wouldn't care about anything I said.

Scott spoke to me on and off. How did I like Lincoln? What was my best subject? What was it like having a father who was an English professor?

Conversation was just short of painful. Scott must have thought I was a real jerk. He'd probably never look twice at me again, I thought. Mercifully the bell rang.

Those had been the longest forty-two minutes of my life! I felt like a total moron, just sitting there. No witty or scintillating comments had crossed my lips the entire time. I had never been so alone in a crowd! So, the Daltonites and I would part ways. Worse things had happened, I tried to console myself.

I gathered up my books quickly. Ginger smiled. She was the only one. Everybody else had melted into a single unit, filing out of the lunchroom. I longed to talk to Peggy.

Scott had excused himself to go across the room to talk to a senior, who was on the hockey team. I debated whether I should wait for him to return. My next class, algebra—also my worst class—was as far from the cafeteria as you could get. I always just made it. Algebra was taught by my least favorite teacher, Ms. Burke.

As I stood waiting, I saw a couple of kids pass by Scott and tap him on the shoulder. He was so popular! Just the kind of guy I wanted to go out with—but probably never would. Not after my mute act today. He'd be relieved if I just faded out gracefully.

Which is what I did.

I dashed into algebra just in time to find out I'd flunked the first test. So had Audrey. After class, she said, "Want to study together on Saturday?"

Although she'd asked me, I had a hunch she was as unenthused about the prospect of studying with me as I was with her. On the other hand, with my average I couldn't afford to be picky.

"Why not? We both could use the help. Two heads are better than one."

All through my history class sixth period, I contemplated the wisdom of spending an entire afternoon with Audrey. I finally decided that if neither of us knew anything, we couldn't be much help to each other. I'd have to think of an excuse for getting out of studying with her.

I was always first in oral communications class because it was across the hall from history. I was surprised to see Scott storm in right after me.

He wasn't happy. Was he angry because I had left the cafeteria? I murmured hello and was about to apologize when he said, "You would not believe how I messed up on my algebra exam! And usually I'm good in math. It's the teacher, you know."

"If it's Ms. Burke, I know. I have her fifth period," I said sympathetically.

"Sixth with me." Other kids filtered in. "Why'd you split from the cafeteria?"

I was aware that everyone who walked in, Ms. Perez included, was looking at Scott, who was standing over my desk. I could feel myself blushing.

Then Scott said, "Oh, I know why!" He grinned. "You have algebra after lunch. That's a trek through the whole school."

I swallowed hard. "Yes." It was nearly time for the warning bell to sound.

"Well, anyway, I wanted to ask you out for Saturday night. There's a Hitchcock festival at the Clarion."

The warning bell coincided with my whispered reply. "That sounds great. I love Hitchcock."

He nodded and walked to his seat. Wow! Scott Holbrook had asked me out! Scott Holbrook was taking me to a Hitchcock festival at the Clarion.

And we'd be *alone.* Not with the others! I knew things would be super if it were just the two of us!

At home that afternoon I called Peggy. I was so excited I could hardly speak. When she did drag the story out of me, she shouted, "Oh, Nina, that's wonderful!"

I could have hugged her. I knew she didn't entirely approve of my associating with Daltonites, yet she was happy for me because I was happy.

A true friend, I thought.

Chapter Three

"How much money do I have left in my If-It's-Important-Enough Fund?"

I settled into a big, lumpy chair my mother had purchased at a flea market. Her den was decorated in FM and GS, Flea Market and Garage Sale. The shelves were lined with books upon books, mainly science fiction and fantasy. Mom had every author from Asimov to Tolkien.

The If-It's-Important-Enough Fund was money my parents doled out. They have this theory that even kids with a regular allowance never really learn budgeting. So, I had no actual money to use, just the fund, which they controlled. We don't always agree on what's truly needed, however. Like last spring when I desperately wanted a strapless, sequined camisole to wear to a rock concert with Peggy.

"You have some money left," Mom said. "But you still need a new winter coat."

"Oh."

"If your face drooped any more, Nina, it would reach the floor." She pushed her eyeglasses up on the bridge of her nose. "It's something extremely special, isn't it?"

"Kind of."

"Nina Ward, what is it?"

"Someone asked me to go to the movies on Saturday night."

Mom jumped up from behind her desk and slammed shut her latest science-fiction novel. She sat on the arm of my lumpy chair. "It's that boy Scott you told me about last night, isn't it? You had lunch with him!"

Honestly, Mom gets like a teenager when boys ask me out. Actually, this is super because lots of girls can't talk to their mothers at all. Peggy's mother isn't even aware Peggy's going steady with Jack. Mrs. Blair is unapproachable about anything except mortgage rates and the price of gas. My mother talks to Peggy whenever she can, but it isn't the same as confiding in her own mother. I quickly filled Mom in on what had happened.

"Well, what's wrong then? It's not because of what I said about the fund, is it?"

"Well, partly. I did want something special—"

"Not that sequined orange camisole?"

"It wasn't orange. It was electric coral."

We laughed. Then Mom said, "But I do think the fund could manage a new sweater or blouse. You do have dressy pants," she reminded me. "Those black ones. And come to think of it, *I* could use some makeup. Would you mind shopping on Friday night with your ancient mom instead of with Peggy? No, I guess it wouldn't be Peggy anyway. She'd be with Jack on a Friday night. I suppose you've made plans with Ginger or Daisy. Do I have the names right?"

"Right as usual. But I'm not going with them," I said, sighing.

"Are you having problems getting to know them, Nina?"

"No. I'm learning all about *them*. They're sophisticated, busy, and they're all lifelong friends. It's me they don't know."

"Then make it your business to open yourself up to them," Mom said matter-of-factly. "I've raised a wonderful, creative, sensitive, and bright daughter. Don't you dare think any less of her than I do!" She hugged me.

"I'll try," I said, feeling revitalized. Mom was right! People liked me. The Daltonites couldn't be *that* different. *Could they*?

* * *

I told Audrey at school the next day that I wouldn't be able to study with her Saturday. I told her I had a date that night and I'd be too busy getting ready.

Then at lunch I marched over to the Daltonites' table. The reason for my boldness was simple—Scott was already there, an empty seat next to him. He expected me. Ginger seemed pleased to see me, too.

"I missed you by our lockers this morning. My father had a client in Maitland, so I drove in with him. I thought we'd be early, but there was a big accident on the interstate."

I was about to say I'd wondered where she'd been when Daisy piped up, "Anyone hurt? Remember that wreck Wendie had last August when that beer truck rear-ended her? What a mess! And it wasn't even her fault!"

So, I didn't get a word in. They were off discussing Wendie. I drifted into my own thoughts. Ginger's father had a client in Maitland. I assumed her father was either a lawyer or an accountant. I wanted to ask her but didn't want to interrupt the talk flow.

I wondered if Scott had told his friends he'd asked me out. Since they were all so close, I figured he must have at least mentioned it in passing. But no one said anything about it, not even Ginger, who was the nicest to me. Did they disapprove of his dating an outsider? I sipped orange juice. They might; they were such a close-knit group. In fact, the word "snobs" surfaced in my thoughts at one point, but I brushed it aside. There was another possibility. What if Scott had been reluctant to tell them? Or thought it wasn't even worth mentioning? No! That was silly! He wouldn't have asked me out if he felt that way. So, I was back to square one. He had probably informed the others, and they disapproved. I made a vow to speak up.

But beyond telling Ginger I loved her emerald green sweater, I didn't have a chance to contribute to the general conversation. Since the dialogue was mainly concerned with Marty's football game and Wendie's birthday party sometime in October, I was really left out of things. To my delight, Scott rescued me—even if he didn't realize he'd done so. He talked about hockey.

I told him Rory O'Toole had been over to my house the other night for a conference with my father. Scott's eyes widened at that. I didn't explain that Rory called me the Muppet, meaning I was cute but not to be taken seriously. Or that Rory was only interested in his glorious reflection in our hall mirror.

No, I couldn't bare the truth to Scott. He

clearly worshiped Rory O'Toole. Instead, I said, "Wait until I tell Rory I'm friends with Scott Holbrook. He'll be impressed." Actually, he'd probably ask me who Scott was, but it was only a little white lie, and it brought the widest grin to Scott's gorgeous face. Who could it hurt?

Chapter Four

Mom and I spent over two hours at the mall Friday night. I found a gorgeous silk blouse—on sale, no less—within five minutes of stepping into Bloomingdale's. I also bought a silver cameo to pin on the high collar of the blouse.

We took two hours because of Mom. I explained it to my father. "First, she was insanely jealous of the fabulous buy I got on my blouse, so I had to take her into the ladies' room so she wouldn't break down in public. When she calmed down, I marched her over to the misses' blouses, where she took twenty-seven minutes to find *the* perfect top to wear on your anniversary in December. I have been sworn to secrecy as to what it looks like, but I will warn you that you'd better wear sunglasses because sequins and rhinestone studs can be blinding." Actually, Mom bought a silver lamé tunic, but my version was more dramatic.

"Then we went to the jewelry department. I picked out my cameo quickly, but not fast enough. The cosmetics department is directly across from jewelry, and there your wife, my mother, decided she wanted a 'new look.' During the next twenty-seven minutes, Mom had her entire face redone—"

"Nina!" Mom interrupted, laughing. "You make it sound like plastic surgery! The woman merely put on some new foundation and blusher. And didn't she give you tips on how to make your eyes look bigger?"

"Cynthia, let her finish," Dad said. "I wish Tim were here. He's missing one of her better stories. You'll have to tell him this one the next time you baby-sit for the twins—which is on Zelda and Tim's anniversary next month, I believe."

I smiled. It was easy to talk to my folks, to Peggy and the other kids I've known all my life, and maybe even Scott. But the other Daltonites? They seemed above this sort of thing. What was a little shopping trip compared to large, catered parties and huge houses on the beach and accidents with beer trucks? I dismissed such negative thoughts from my head and concentrated on good feelings.

* * *

On Saturday Peggy called twice to ask what I was wearing. I was glad to talk to her. She was as excited about my date as I was. She even came over in the middle of the afternoon and made me model my outfit for her. She gave me her seal of approval, but still I was beginning to get nervous, very nervous.

My life was so dull. Could I possibly make it sound glamorous enough to impress a Daltonite?

I began to experience butterflies and the worst case of sweaty palms I'd had since I first skated backward on ice skates. If I remembered correctly, I had crashed into the wall. Would I crash on my date?

No! I pushed my limp hair away from my face. Maybe if I piled it on top of my head, it would give me some needed height. I fixed it in a loose chignon. It looked good! Why hadn't I thought of it before?

I was so engrossed in wondering what Scott and I would talk about that I didn't hear the bell ring. When Mom knocked on my door and told me Scott was downstairs, the butterfly attack resumed. I ran into the bathroom, gulped some cool water. Then, taking a deep breath, I walked downstairs.

Scott and Dad were standing by the enormous bay window, and Dad was pointing out to the lawn. I had no clue what they were discussing. Scott looked terribly handsome in a gray turtleneck and a black blazer with charcoal pants.

"Hello there, remember me?" I said. "What's so fascinating outside?"

Scott whirled. A gleam entered his eyes. "I think everything fascinating just entered this room."

"Oh, he's a charmer," Mom whispered. She'd followed me down.

"We were looking at the spruces," Dad said. "Scott wanted to know whether we put lights on them for Christmas. His father does the lighting for the malls in the area."

"Oh, no!" I feigned mock horror. "Your dad is the one to blame for the pink trees and purple elves that glow in magenta light?"

"Well, sort of. Actually, my father runs the company. He doesn't do the actual lighting. He just collects the profits." He grinned. "Are you ready, Nina? The bus leaves in ten minutes."

"All set." I glanced at my parents, who were now sitting together on the living room sofa. "Twelve-thirty, OK?"

"We'll probably take in a pizza, too, Mr. Ward. The bus runs every hour at that time. We could be a little late."

"Twelve-thirty, one. If you miss the bus, just give us a call. I'll be burning the midnight oil going over assignments."

Dad spoke firmly, but I could tell that both he and Mom were impressed with Scott. Who wouldn't be? I just hoped Scott was equally impressed with me.

The walk to the bus stop was a quiet one. It was as if we really wanted to get involved in a conversation but couldn't think of anything except, "Nice night. Real warm." When we reached the stop, I said, "We've exhausted the weather, unless you're considering a career in meteorology."

Scott laughed, and that broke the ice. We didn't stop talking all through the ride. He warned me that the original version of *The Man Who Knew Too Much*, one of the Hitchcock films we were going to see, was scarier than the Doris Day-Jimmy Stewart version.

"You've seen both?"

The crowded bus lurched into the mall. "I'm a Hitchcock freak. There are hardly any of his films I haven't seen." We stood up and began walking down the aisle. "They're supposed to have a marathon of them on TV sometime in November. The whole gang will be over at my house. You'll like it."

I had to be careful not to trip getting off the

bus. November was over a month away. He thought we'd still be together then!

We had to wait in line to get into the theater. Although the customers consisted mainly of college kids, there was a sprinkling of kids from Lincoln. I recognized a few, and Scott waved to one couple and whispered to me, "That's Dave Marini. He's a senior. He's on the team."

Dave and his girlfriend smiled at me. Scott had taken my hand when we'd gotten off the bus, as if it were the most natural gesture in the world. By the time we walked a few steps, it was. Now, two poised-looking seniors were acknowledging me. It was too incredible for words!

The movies were wonderful. And Scott was right. The original *The Man Who Knew Too Much* was much spookier than the updated version.

The show let out after eleven, and we walked over to Sal's Pizzeria, *the* place to go in the mall. "Looks like everybody had the same idea," Scott shouted over the din of voices and blaring rock music.

We found a table quickly, though, as a mob of college kids who'd occupied four tables left. Scott asked me what I wanted on the pizza, and I told him mushrooms. So he ordered a large pie, half with mushrooms and half with double everything, and two large Cokes.

While we waited for the pie, Scott started a discussion of the movies, and our mouths were off and running. By the time the pizza arrived, we were glad just to sit and quietly pig out. After we'd each polished off a slice, I asked Scott about the hockey season.

"Do you really think you'll get to be captain? Oh, I don't mean I don't believe you can—just, I mean you're a sophomore and all."

Scott smiled, reached over the table, and pressed his hand on mine. "Nina, let's just say if I don't, my friends will probably organize a boycott. They're very, very loyal."

"I've noticed."

"I have a pretty good shot at becoming captain," he said, sipping his Coke. "Dave, the guy who was in line with us, is the current captain. He's giving it up because he's graduating in January and won't be around for the whole season. He'll nominate his successor."

"You!" I nibbled on the next slice of pie.

"I hope so. Dave's very concerned about the Roadrunners. He wants a real leader out there. And I was the captain of the Dalton squad—"

"Boy, you sure don't brag, do you? You

scored a hat trick against Maitland and a *double* hat trick against the St. Mary's team. That's really something."

"You seem to know a lot about me, Nina," he said softly, touching my hand again.

"Mmmm." I could barely swallow the pie.

"I intend to learn a lot about you."

I gulped, and my hand—the one he wasn't holding—shook. What a fabulous evening! And it wasn't over yet. We still had food to finish, a bus ride home, and who knew what at the door? My thoughts flew to that special moment. Once, in ninth grade, a kid named Bobby Danbury had given me a few quick, embarrassed pecks on my cheek. Scott's kiss would be dreamy and lingering and—

"We were wondering where you two had gotten to!"

My sweet reverie was rudely interrupted by Marty's booming voice. "We even hung around the Clarion to see when the show let out. We un-intellectual types go for Burt Reynolds movies!"

A collective guffaw arose from Wendie, Ginger, Ace, Daisy, and Duane, who was in my algebra class. Within seconds they corralled another table, put it next to ours, ordered three pies, several more sodas, and rapidly flew into their usual conversation. I felt like an unwanted anchovy. Why couldn't Scott have been part of my crowd so we could go out with Peggy and Jack? No, I told myself firmly, you've got to make new friends. Ginger slid in next to me.

"Your hair looks terrific," she said. "You should wear it like that more often."

"Thanks," I murmured. "And I like your sweater," I added.

Why couldn't I think of something more original or intelligent to say? I had no trouble when it was just Scott and me. I might not have been witty and hilarious, but we held a conversation. Now he was talking to Wendie and Marty. Suddenly he glanced my way. If I failed to contribute to the conversation, not only would this evening be over quickly, but maybe so would the chance for future dates with Scott. His friends were terribly important to him. "Loyal." That had been his own description.

"I think Ginger looks like a model," Ace suddenly said.

"She should be a model," Wendie chimed in. Wendie was pretty and reminded me of Elizabeth Taylor in *National Velvet*, a favorite movie of mine when I was ten and horse crazy. But the Daltonites wouldn't be interested in that sort of comment.

"Ginger has what it takes," Ace said, putting his arm around her.

"I don't know," Ginger said slowly. "Posing all the time, having to be constantly 'on.' That's not my style."

"Oh, you could swing it," Daisy said as the waitress put down their pizzas. "Hey, get this—guess who *claims* to be a model?"

"Who?" Everyone said in unison.

"That tubby kid in oral communications. What's-her-face?"

Ace replied, "Audrey Van."

"Yeah, she's the one. That blob claims she models. Can you believe it? I was in the bathroom, and there she was, applying lip gloss with a brush and making faces in the mirror. Said she was practicing for the camera. I almost died."

I don't know why I did it. Maybe it had something to do with loyalty. Audrey Van wasn't a good friend, but we'd known each other for seven years. Besides, I wanted to set Daisy straight.

"She does model," I said. The Daltonites all became quiet. "Audrey is an outsize model. Chubby clothes," I added when Scott gave me a quizzical glance. "She's been doing it for about a year. She took lessons. Still does. She models in department stores. Last summer she worked in a show at Lane Bryant in New York City. She invited a bunch of us from Maitland to watch her. It was fantastic!" I was on a roll now. They were all attentive. "She was simply marvelous! I helped her with her changes. It took some trouble to get me into the wings," I said, hoping that was the correct word. "But she needed me for moral support. It really was fun! She's done ads, too. She'll have a big one in the spring issue of *Young People on Parade.*" I knew Audrey had been in an ad for Easter clothes in a Pennsylvania newspaper. Her next shots *could* be for *Young People on Parade.* You never knew. And spring was a long way off. The kids would forget my colorful tale by then. Anyhow, it felt good to stop Daisy's catty remarks.

Daisy was the first to speak. "Really? Who'd have believed it? I thought she was putting me on." I noticed a definite icy edge to Daisy's voice and wondered if it was a good idea to have spoken up.

"Do you go into the city much?" Ginger asked.

"Fairly often," I said, aware that they were hanging on my words. "My uncle Timothy, he's the one with the two sets of twins—"

"The Bobbsey twins!" Marty laughed. "What?" Wendie asked.

"Oh," said Marty, "Nina told this funny story about them in oral communications."

I grinned. Scott squeezed my hand. "Uncle Timothy is in advertising, and he thinks I have a future in that field. He's always asking me to come into the city and visit his office. I went about six times this summer." Actually, only once, but he did insist I had a career in advertising.

"I love going into the city," Ginger said. "Hey, why don't we go in sometime?"

"Sometime?" I said, praying my voice didn't catch.

"Like next Saturday?" Ginger asked.

"That sounds su—" I started to say, but Scott's voice cut me off.

"No."

I could have died of embarrassment. How could I have been so dumb? Taking it for granted Scott would want to see me again next Saturday.

"I have hockey practice on Saturday. Can we go on Sunday? Is that OK with you, Nina?"

I smiled. Plans flew in every direction. Wendie, Marty, Daisy, and Duane couldn't make it since they had tickets to the Meadowlands for a Giants football game. But in a matter of minutes, it was settled that Ace, Ginger, Scott, and I would have a fantastic outing in New York City the following Sunday. I knew about a great Chinese restaurant, and Ginger wanted to do regular old sight-seeing.

Ginger turned to me. "Why don't you come over to my house Saturday morning? We can make more plans then."

I nodded happily. Or was it deliriously? Ace drove us to my house and waited while Scott walked me to the door. At the door Scott grasped my shoulders gently. He leaned over and kissed my forehead. Then he removed one hand from my shoulder and tilted my chin upward. After planting a soft kiss on my lips, he said, "We'll do this better when we don't have an audience."

Chapter Five

I stayed in bed late Sunday morning, listening to the sparrows chirp in the maple tree outside my bedroom window and enjoying the hum of Dad's food processor as he prepared his "Sunday morning surprise." Everything seemed super, great, fantastic, and just absolutely fabulous!

I turned over on my stomach. Scott liked me. Scott Holbrook, a Daltonite, and me, a mere Maitlander. I was already contemplating what to wear on our next date, knowing full well that the fund would not be available again. A trip to the city required a nice outfit. I had a dark green, long-sleeved wool dress I'd worn last Thanksgiving and Christmas. But would it be too warm for the beginning of October? I could ask Ginger what she'd be wearing.

I twisted and sat up, thinking of my success of the night before—the whole Dalton gang had been impressed with my telling of Audrey's modeling career. OK, I admitted, throwing my legs over the side of the bed, the telling hadn't been precisely accurate, but who was to know I hadn't attended the Lane Bryant show? They wouldn't check up on it.

My heart galloped for a second. Would they? Would Daisy confront Audrey and demand, "Was Nina Ward with you at the fashion show?" I shook my head. No! Of course not. Daisy couldn't bother herself with Audrey. Besides, while my tale had amused the kids, it wasn't something they'd remember for all time. They'd forget about it by lunch on Monday.

But instead of reassuring me, that little thought caused the galloping to start again. If they forgot, I'd have to impress them all over again! How? No brilliant thoughts occurred to me. And if I dwelt on that thought too much, all the good feelings about the night before would dwindle. I wanted to remain floaty for a while longer.

Determined not to think anymore about it, I grabbed my robe and went downstairs. My parents were nice and did not ask questions about the date. Contrary to Dad's comment to Scott, he hadn't been "burning the midnight oil" when I came home. My parents had gone to bed. And this morning, they said nothing, waiting for me to make the first move. After sampling one of Dad's strawberry tarts—the surprise—I said casually, "I had a super time. We're all going into the city next week." That required some additional explaining.

When I finished, Dad said, "I don't know this Ace person. If he's going to drive you, I'd like to meet him."

"But he drove me home last night. Oh, I guess I forgot to say that," I added when they raised their eyebrows. "I was home on time. Besides, having to meet him is positively archaic!"

"If it is, I'm afraid I'll have to join the fossils, too, Nina," Mom said, stirring honey into her herbal tea. "We don't know these new friends of yours. You can't go unless we meet him first."

"But you know Scott. You liked him. Ace is his friend!"

"That doesn't mean anything," Dad said. "Can't you invite Ace over one day? We could check him out then."

It was as if my glorious date had never occurred. I could just see it now. "Ace, please come over to my house to meet my folks.

They want to make sure you possess a legal driver's license. And would you mind taking a breathalizer test before you drive me into the city?"

What would he think? First, he'd collapse into hysterics, and then he'd ask if he should bring a high chair along for me. Scott would probably consider me a baby, too. Maybe I could get Ace over here without his knowing he was being checked out. How could I do that? What sort of story could I invent?

When I finally came up with something, it was totally by accident. Ace gave his oral communications report on Tuesday, and it was the content of his speech that triggered my idea. His most exciting summer day was the evening he and a whole bunch of other people in coastal New Jersey reported seeing mysterious lights off the shore. It had been in all the papers. Scientists claimed it was a meteor shower, but plenty of people, Ace included, believed the lights could've been UFOs. From that, I realized Ace Turner was a science-fiction fan.

When class let out, I waited for Ginger and Ace. Scott was with me. Ever since the day he had asked me out, we had walked out of the building together.

"Ace," I said, "I was thinking, if you like

sci-fi stuff maybe you'd like to meet my mother. She's had a few science-fiction stories printed." Actually, she had one published last year, and another was due for publication this summer. She also had a very large stack of rejections.

"What magazines?" Ace asked. I told him. He beamed.

"Listen, why don't you and Ginger stop by my house this evening? You, too, Scott," I said, hoping it didn't sound like an afterthought, which it certainly wasn't.

"I can't. We're starting practice, and I have to meet with the coach afterward. I'll be lucky to get the six o'clock bus back to the shore."

"Why don't you come straight over to my house from practice and have dinner with us?"

"Yeah, Scott, then Ginger and I could pick you up and drive you home. Come on, I want to meet a real soul mate."

It was settled. Now I had to tell my parents that there'd be one more for dinner and two more stopping by later. They took it nicely. The meat loaf, macaroni and cheese, and green beans were items that could be easily stretched. Dad even went out for a loaf of french bread.

"If Scott's anything like Rory, he'll be starving after practice."

Rory O'Toole! Would Scott ask Dad about him? Dad's replies wouldn't match the glowing compliments I'd given Scott about Rory. I had to steer the conversation away from that subject.

It was easier than I thought because Scott literally dragged himself into my house. Although he'd showered before leaving school, his usually neat hair was messy, his eyes half-closed, and he kept rubbing his shoulders.

"First practice of the season always does this to me. Wow! What smells so good?" When I told him, he smiled. "Sounds super."

And it was. Because he was exhausted, he didn't have much to say. Mostly we listened to Mom's entertaining description of the library regulars. I'd heard it a dozen times, but Scott hadn't. There are certain people who haunt the library because they don't have any other place to go. There's one blue-haired woman who reads every mystery novel five times; a young, unemployed teacher who reads magazines and stares out the window; and the Golfer, a middle-aged man in Brooks Brothers' suits, who comes in twice a week toting his golf clubs. He borrows books on archaeology and divorce. Then there's the woman who reserves every bestseller and returns it the following day, always saying, "Ugh, this was dreadful." Then she reserves more bestsellers. I don't think Scott's full attention was on the stories, but he listened politely and smiled in the right places. My heart went out to him. He was totally wiped out!

He offered to help load the dishwasher, but Mom and I said, "No, that's OK," in unison, and we all laughed. I ushered him into the living room while Dad retired to his den to work on a lecture.

"This is really nice," Scott said, sitting on the sofa. "Quiet. Not like my house."

"Your place is noisy?"

"It gets that way. I have two younger sisters and an older brother. He's away at college but comes home most weekends. It gets particularly loud then."

Funny how I hadn't known about his family life. We talked a lot but never about that. We still had so much to discover about each other!

He leaned closer to me and slowly, deliciously, planted a soft kiss on my lips. I responded. The kisses grew deeper. Then suddenly we broke apart, taking quick breaths. I'd never felt so utterly wonderful. He reached for me again, but common sense entered my head.

My parents could walk in at any moment. Fortunately, Ace and Ginger arrived just then. My parents wandered in, and I could tell they liked Ginger and Ace immediately.

Ace and Mom hit it off, talking about recent science-fiction books they'd read. Ginger rolled her eyes. "The stuff he goes for is too weird for me. I like love stories and Gothics. I'm crazy about romantic suspense."

"So am I!"

"I read *Sports Illustrated.* Is that romantic or suspenseful?" Scott asked from his perch on the couch.

Ginger and I looked at each other, nodded, grabbed throw pillows, and smacked him with them.

Ginger started talking about her favorite suspense writers, and we found we read the same ones. "I have a huge collection of paperbacks. I'll lend you whatever you want when you come over Saturday."

"Fantastic. I'm especially looking forward to seeing the gazebo, though."

"The high point of the Callison Homestead Tour."

We laughed. Ace and Mom returned. He had a copy of her published story clutched in his hand. He said he'd give her a review of it.

She said, "You can do that when you pick up Nina to go into the city on Sunday."

I would have cheered, but a peculiar noise from the sofa stopped me. Scott sat there head thrown back, eyes shut, mouth ajar, snoring steadily. Ginger was the only one who understood when I said, "Now, that's romantic."

Chapter Six

Rain pounded on my umbrella as I walked to school on Friday. I spotted three figures huddled at the corner. The tall, athletic form belonged to Peggy, the gaunt figure to Jack Adams, and the surprisingly tall body to Bobby Danbury, my klutzy ninth-grade fling. Bobby used to be short, but over the summer he shot up so fast he didn't seem used to his new height. He reminded me of a marionette.

"You know, I have Ms. Perez first period," Bobby said when the four of us began walking. "I gave a speech on learning CPR from the local paramedics. After class she said I'd given the best talk in her first-period class and that Nina Ward had been the best speaker in her other sophomore group."

"That's nice. Oral communications is my favorite subject."

"Mine, too. Ms. Perez wants to recommend

us for the special Thanksgiving assembly and for spots on the debate team. Imagine that! I expected you to give good speeches, Nina, but me, the stutterer himself?"

Bobby had worked hard to overcome his bad stutter. He'd attended special classes and taken plenty of abuse from cruel kids. Now he only stuttered when he tried to talk too fast. I was impressed he'd given such a super speech.

"You expected me to give a good report?" I asked when we reached school. I looked for the Dalton bus, but it wasn't in sight. The rainstorm probably had slowed traffic.

"Sure, you have a natural way of speaking."

"She's got a big mouth, you mean," Peggy said dryly. "The highways are flooded," she added. "I doubt *they'll* make it until second or third period. I'm sorry. That sounded terrible. I just miss seeing you since you're with them so much."

"We have to keep in touch more," I agreed. "Let's get together one day after school real soon." She smiled and said she'd love that. I watched her dash up the steps, agile and effortless. She reminded me of Daisy, the way she moved. Peggy would never see the resemblance, though. Neither would Daisy, for that matter.

My best friend was right. The Dalton bus didn't arrive until third period. At lunch, the tale of the bus ride was the number-one topic of conversation.

"I swear the water was past those huge wheels." Daisy said, shivering. "Why can't they build a school on the shore instead of forcing us to ride in that bus?"

"Money, dear Daisy," Ace said. "Not everyone is loaded, you know, especially not the county government. I kind of enjoyed the ride today. I thought I'd have a chance to practice my Olympic swimming style."

"They allow belly flops in the Olympics now!" Marty said, and everybody broke up.

"In the winter we'll probably have a lot of schoolless days when the snows hit," Ace said.

"What a shame," said Daisy sarcastically.

"Don't say that, man!" Scott groaned. "I have hockey games to get to!"

"Then you can skate in," Duane said.

"Or I could stay over at Nina's."

Hoots of laughter, and I blushed. When the bell rang and I made my usual mad dash for the door in order to reach Ms. Burke's class on time, Scott touched my arm. "I'm sorry."

"Sorry?"

"For embarrassing you before. Saying I could spend the night at your house. I saw you blush. You look adorable when you blush. But I'm still sorry."

"Oh, you didn't embarrass me. Well, not much," I added, laughing. "Just don't say that kind of thing in front of my parents. They might take you seriously."

"Don't worry. I want your folks to approve of me." He leaned over and kissed me. Again, redness crept to the collar of my heather turtleneck. Kids kissed in the halls all the time. But it was a first for me!

I ran all the way to algebra and managed to do OK on a surprise quiz. When class was over, Daisy hurried over to me. "I passed! I know I did! Miracle of miracles!"

To say I was taken aback by Daisy's effusive outburst was an understatement. Although we shared algebra class, she never joined me in my mad rush from the cafeteria to the room. Nor did she ever address me without the other Daltonites around, which worried me since she clearly had a great deal of influence with the group.

"I'll walk with you to history."

We shared that class, too, and she'd never accompanied me there either. If I had any qualms about holding up my end of the conversation, I shouldn't have worried. She talked enough for both of us. She complained about the ride to school again and said how lucky I was to live in Maitland. "You can walk to school."

"Tramping through the rain this morning was not exactly fun. When the wind came up, I would've loved to have been in a bus, even one with submerged tires."

She laughed. Too brightly? Too loudly? A signal went off in my head. She was up to something. That had to be the reason for this sudden display of friendship.

"Your friends live nearby, too, don't they?" she asked when we reached Mr. Weinberg's history class.

"Yes, some of them do."

"I don't know the Maitland kids that well, but Wendie—she's my best friend—is getting acquainted with some of them. She has Ms. Perez first period."

A warning beep sounded in my brain. Ms. Perez, first period. Where had I heard this before?

"Wendie said this Maitland kid, um, what's his name?" Daisy tapped her long nails on her loose-leaf. "Bobby somebody? Cute, blond, with freckles?"

"Danbury," I said, slipping into my seat.

"Whatever. Wendie said he gave a fabulous speech. I think it's nice that the two of you,

you and this Bobby, are friends. You'll be over at Ginger's this weekend, won't you?"

My head spun. I couldn't figure out what she was driving at; yet a nagging inner voice warned me it could be trouble.

"Tell Ginger *all* about Bobby. She'll be very, very interested." And Daisy winked as the second bell rang.

Why would Ginger Callison want to know about Bobby Danbury of all people?

Chapter Seven

That question hounded me all Saturday morning as I traveled down to the shore. Not many passengers were on the nine o'clock bus as it lumbered along the highway. One of the rear windows refused to close, and blasts of chilly air whistled through. I tugged at the drawstring of my green windbreaker, pulling the zipper all the way to my neck. Ginger had said we'd walk along the beach, so I'd dressed casually in jeans, Nikes, and a navy sweatshirt.

The driver let me off near Sandstone Drive, Ginger's street. As I walked along, pungent ocean air stung my nostrils. The grayness of the Atlantic Ocean loomed before me. What a view! Through the semibarren trees, I caught a glimpse of secluded, gabled houses. Which was the Callison house? She lived at 10 Sandstone Drive. She said I couldn't miss it. And she was right.

Ginger's house faced the beach. It was barricaded from the water by a high stone wall. I climbed dozens of steps until I reached the front door of the old multigabled, Victorian-style house.

On my first ring Ginger opened the door and waved me in. She was wearing faded jeans and a kelly green sweatshirt that was dotted with dust. Her beautiful hair was stuck up with a lone barrette. "I'm sorry I couldn't meet the bus. I had to clean my room. My mother won't allow me to do anything on Saturday until my room is clean. Do you have to do that, too?"

"Yeah, if my room isn't spotless on the weekends, Mom takes Polaroid shots of it and hangs them on the porch for the Board of Health to see."

Ginger giggled. We entered the hallway. Morning light filtered through an eastern window making the Oriental throw rugs and dark wood spring to life. Mrs. Callison was in the living room dusting. Ginger introduced us. Even in a well-worn plaid housedress, her mother was as attractive as Ginger, and she was just as nice. She greeted me warmly and said we'd have a chat later in the day.

Then Ginger and I walked to her second-floor bedroom. It was twice the size of mine and filled with antique furniture, including twin beds. "I have friends stay over a lot. I hope you can do that sometime soon."

"Me, too," I said, plopping on one bed.

She put on a cassette, and music filled the room. "I have some things planned. Like lots of food, a walk on the beach, *and* a surprise around four. No fair asking!" She wagged a finger. "You can stay until after four, can't you?"

"Sure. But you left out the gazebo. I really want to see that."

"An oversight. I told you, it's the high point of the tour! I hope you're not disappointed, though. It's not in the greatest condition. Do you like this tape?"

We got into a big discussion of our favorite performers. She was floored when I told her I'd seen the Stones at Madison Square Garden. "My uncle Timothy managed tickets through his ad agency somehow, so Peggy and I went."

"Peggy?"

"Peggy Blair, she's from Maitland." And so was Bobby Danbury. Why hadn't she asked about him? "Peg is my best friend."

"I don't know her, but if you're close, I'm sure she's a terrific person."

If only Peggy would say the same about you! I thought.

"Tell me about the concert."

I did. In my own fashion. Not that Mick Jagger and company needed any embellishments, but the trip there and back certainly did. "We were supposed to be in by twelve-thirty, but we didn't make it. The concert didn't even let out until close to midnight. Luckily, Peggy's parents didn't wait up for us. I stayed over at her house that night."

"What do you mean, 'luckily'? What happened?" Ginger asked, taking off the cassette and inserting a more appropriate Stones tape.

"What didn't? A bunch of kids asked us to go to SoHo in lower Manhattan. They had some friends who had this loft." Everything was true right up to this point. The thing was the smell of booze on the kids' breaths and the aroma of grass surrounding them were enough to send Peggy and me back to New Jersey pronto. However, in the version to Ginger, "We went to the loft and . . ." I rolled my eyes. Now, I could tell Ginger that Peggy and I joined this imaginary party, and she'd think Peggy and I were *very, very* wild, or I could tell her we cut out, scared out of our wits, which might make her think we were babies. I thought fast.

"We ambled into this marijuana haze, and a guy wandered over to us. Just an ordinary guy except for this boa constrictor wrapped around his shoulders—"

"Auggh! Just like Alice Cooper! I hate snakes!"

"So do Peggy and I. And we weren't crazy about being in a room we couldn't even see through. We wanted fun, not trouble. So we left. But then we were alone in SoHo, and we got lost."

Ginger was a rapt audience as my tale of prowling through narrow streets and spotting danger lurking at every darkened corner grew and grew. Finally, I got Peggy and me back to New Jersey. "It was so late that we had to sneak in, which was not easy since Peggy's bedroom is on the second floor. We ended up stacking garbage cans, and believe me, it is difficult to tell garbage cans not to clank together."

Ginger laughed.

"OK, so we finally got them fixed and climbed to the window. And there sat Damien, Peg's overweight Angora cat, blocking our entry. He is not a cat to fool around with."

"Then how'd you get inside?"

"Quick thinking"—which I was doing a lot

of in this story. "I remembered seeing an empty can of cat food in the garbage cans. Just the sight of it got Damien off the sill. We finally made it inside, and nobody was any worse for the experience—except Damien, who was angry."

"Such exciting things happen to you! You've got to tell the others about this! At Wendie's party."

There was a momentary silence as the cassette stopped. "I don't know if this is of any great importance, but I wasn't invited. I really don't know Wendie that well. I only met her at the pizzeria that one night," I added, hoping that was the reason but not believing it.

"Oh, Nina. It's not what you think. Wendie can't invite you because she doesn't know about it. It's a surprise. It'll be held here. What's wrong? Oh, wait a minute—don't tell me. The great hockey player neglected to invite you." She shook her head. "He's so involved with hockey, he forgets everything else. Trust me. He'll ask you."

I smiled and prayed she was right! I also saw an opportunity to find out about Daisy's cryptic remarks. "Who'll be your date?"

"Ace. That's a strange question."

"Oh, I thought maybe you dated other guys."

"What? Come on, Nina. You're leading up to something. Out with it!"

"Bobby Danbury," I hedged. "I got the impression you're—you're interested in him."

"Who's Bobby Danbury?"

"You don't know him?" I asked.

"Wait a second. Is he tall with blond hair and freckles?"

"Yeah," I said, utterly confused by now. Why didn't she know him better? "That's him—so you know him?"

"When you've had a person described to you as many times as he's been described to me, you 'know' the person."

The light dawned. "No wonder Daisy acted so strangely!" Quickly I filled Ginger in on what Daisy had said. "I thought *you* were interested in Bobby, which didn't make sense to me since you and Ace seem to be so tight."

"We are. Daisy's the one who's after this Bobby. I guess she was afraid to ask you directly—"

"Daisy afraid? Of me?"

"Don't be fooled by her flippant act. Oh, she *is* catty and sarcastic, but she's really not a bad person. We all love her." Again, speaking for the group—all for one and one for all. "Daisy's a little mixed up now and then. She was probably embarrassed to admit to you that she had her eye on a boy you know better than she does. But she wanted to make sure you passed on any available information about him to me, so I could fill her in."

Daisy and Bobby, I thought. Incredible. I'd have to steer Daisy away from Bobby. For his sake. He'd get all nervous around such a sexy girl and start stuttering. Then she'd make her usual snide remarks. No way Bobby could handle that—or Daisy!

However, I forgot about Bobby and Daisy as the day wore on. Ginger and I found loads of things to discuss. We also devoured a huge lunch, and I met Ginger's hairy Samoyeds, Igor and Ivan, and her brothers, Darrell and Lawrence. They went to Princeton, were cordial and handsome, and didn't treat me like a Muppet, the way Rory did. *Some* college boys could be decent!

Later in the afternoon Ginger and I strolled up from the beach to a small, hidden path that led to the rear of the expansive Callison property. "I hope you won't be too disappointed by the gazebo, Nina. It's sort of dilapidated."

As she uttered those words, the gazebo appeared in front of us. True, the paint was chipped badly, and a few rust spots showed on the iron, but the structure was exactly as I'd imagined from all the Gothic novels I'd read. It was hexagonal in shape, with lacy grillwork stemming from each pillar. The iron curls reached the twelve-foot ceiling, and the roof formed a perfect point. "I love it," I said breathlessly.

We walked inside. A stone bench sat in the middle, and all around the sides a small ledge jutted out, just wide enough for someone to sit on to enjoy the view. "I just love it."

"You said that already!" But I could tell she was pleased. She loved this place, too. I wondered if all the Daltonites did. She seemed to read my mind.

"Ace thinks it's corny. He has no romance in him. Most of the others are so used to it, they don't see it as special. Most, but not all."

I was about to ask her who else thought it was special when Igor and Ivan bounded into the gazebo. Ginger glanced at her watch. "It's four. My brothers deserted them before feeding time. I'd better feed them."

"I'll help," I said, casting a longing glance around the gazebo.

"No, you stay here and enjoy. When you get tired of the atmosphere, come back to the house."

Ginger and the dogs ran back to the house. I sat on the bench for a moment, then wandered over to a pillar. Resting my head against the grillwork, I lovingly touched the iron. Such a romantic setting. How could anyone not appreciate it? "It's absolutely perfect," I said softly.

"I agree."

I whirled around and nearly tripped over the center bench. I'd been so lost in day-dreams, I hadn't heard anyone come up the path. But there he was, his dark hair curving around the collar of his blue bomber jacket, his deep gray eyes staring intently into mine. "Ginger thought you'd be surprised."

Four o'clock. The surprise. The dogs weren't hungry! They'd signaled the arrival of the surprise.

"Ace picked me up at practice. Even if we couldn't have a *real* date today, I wanted to see you. I couldn't wait until tomorrow."

He reached out and drew me to him. His arms felt so strong around my back. We kissed softly, then more deeply. After we broke apart, he took me over to the bench. "I love this place, too," Scott said. "It's kind of hard for some people to understand, you know? Guys aren't supposed to go for romantic settings, but I do. This is special. Almost mysterious."

"Perfect," I said, nuzzling my head against his broad shoulder.

"And our place from now on. Our special place. OK?"

OK! But I had no opportunity to answer as his lips met mine again.

Chapter Eight

Indian summer appeared on Sunday morning. It was sixty-eight degrees when I tumbled out of bed.

"I'll sweat to death in my green dress," I moaned as Dad piled sausages and an omelet on my plate. "Can I borrow your 'He-Man, He Needs It' deodorant?"

"You can't be serious," Mom said, pouring coffee into her mug. "You don't expect to wear that wool dress today?"

"What else?"

Dad stopped serving, and Mom stopped pouring. Dad said, "Doesn't our daughter have a closet filled with blouses, jeans, and skirts, all of which we've been getting the bills for?"

Mom nodded solemnly.

"You're not taking me seriously! I can't wear a summer outfit into New York City in October. It isn't done!"

"Where have I heard that pronouncement before?" Dad muttered.

"Probably from Zelda," Mom answered, adding sugar to her coffee. "She won't wear white shoes after Labor Day or velvet after March twenty-first. She's extremely fastidious about such things. And extremely silly."

"She is not!" Zelda is my favorite aunt. Also my only aunt.

"Any woman who names her children Jessica, Jonathan, Jeremiah, and Jillian, and who says the next ones will be Jonah and Jezebel, qualifies as silly," Dad said.

I ignored his remark, even though I saw the truth in it. I also wondered if my aunt was pregnant again. I'd ask her when I babysat for them on their anniversary. "I'm going to the city with three very fashionable people. They will not be wearing cutoffs and peasant blouses."

"Scott would look adorable in a peasant blouse," Mom said, smiling.

I rolled my eyes. "I'm in a terrible predicament, and you're making jokes! I'll be the only person in the city not in fall clothes if I don't wear the wool dress. I'll just have to figure out how not to sweat to death."

While I figured, the temperature climbed to seventy-two. The "He-Man, He Needs It" stick smelled of disinfectant. I tossed it back into the medicine chest. Glumly I stared out the window. This day was important to me. I had to make a good impression.

I was contemplating calling Peggy for a fashion consultation when the phone rang. I dashed into my room. "Can you believe this weather? I had my new velvet suit all set to wear. And suede boots! What am I going to do?"

Ginger Callison, the chic and gorgeous Daltonite, was asking *me* what to wear? I fell on the bed.

After a few minutes of frantic discussion, we each managed to come up with a more appropriate outfit.

Thank goodness Ginger had called! She'd been as nervous as me. Surprising!

Mom approved of my outfit. "That's lovely. Take a sweater in case there's air conditioning."

"It's been taken care of. Ginger said Wendie would lend me a shawl. She's an expert with yarn, and she's made a million."

"Who's Wendie?"

"One of the gang."

"The gang." Mom shook her head. "I seem to recall that a few short weeks ago, you were worried about these sophisticated Daltonites accepting you. Now, they're 'the gang.' Quite a change. I'm happy for you, honey. I knew you'd adjust to them. You're a bright, imaginative girl. You shouldn't be intimidated by others."

I smiled but said nothing. After that speech, how could I admit that the Daltonites still awed me? Their wealth, their fast, exciting lives, their self-assuredness. They gave the impression of not needing anybody. Maybe not even each other. Certainly not me. I knew Wendie was only lending the shawl because Ginger was asking her to. And Daisy was still seemingly unreachable. I constantly worried about saying the wrong thing around her, of reminding her of my dull lower-class life in slow-moving Maitland. I had to forget about all that, though. I had something else to worry about.

At the pizza parlor I'd led the kids to believe New York City was my territory. It wasn't exactly true. I knew the area around Uncle Timothy's ad agency and east to the East River, and I was familiar with the Central Park region where my aunt and uncle lived, but that was it. Everything other than those points was a mystery. If I'd been smarter, I would've consulted a map of New York City. But I hadn't thought of that brilliant action until just when Ace's bright orange car pulled into the driveway.

After everyone made small talk with my parents, and Ace returned Mom's story with glowing compliments, we headed for the car. Scott said, "I sure hope this restaurant doesn't have a dress code. I have a jacket and tie in the backseat, but I'm not thrilled about wearing them."

A dress code. Did the restaurant have one? Or was it too expensive for high-school kids? Why hadn't I considered these things earlier?

We all got into Ace's car. He sighed. "I wish we were going to the beach."

"Don't you dare wish that!" Ginger said, chiding him. "I'm looking for civilized adventure. Sophisticated happenings. Not volleyball. Sometimes I get so bored with the beach. Here, Nina," she said, handing me a beautifully crocheted shawl. "Wendie wishes she was with us instead of on her way to the Giants game."

"I'd rather go there than to sophisticated adventure and civilized happenings," Ace grumbled, pulling onto the highway.

"I think you have that backward," Scott said, easing his arm around my shoulder. "It's civilized adven—"

"Whatever. How about explaining exactly what it is we're after today?"

Ginger turned to me. "Would you kindly fill these two barbarians in on what I mean? Tell them about the Stones concert."

And I was off and running. Naturally the story changed slightly in the second version. Aware of the fact, I said to Ginger, "I forgot to tell you this part. I mean, so much happened that night!"

"I understand," she said softly.

For a split second, I thought she knew I was stretching the truth. But no, she couldn't.

We parked at a garage on the East Side. It was then I stopped fretting about the cost of the outing. Ace's wallet clearly showed he had enough money for the day. It turned out Scott carried a like amount. I couldn't help but think of Peggy—the Daltonites had money and flaunted it. Oh, well, why not? We were all going to have a great time.

We strolled around the East Side, joined by hundreds of others, who obviously agreed that the day was perfect. We walked by the East River, sparkling in the sunshine. Joggers, old men playing chess, dog walkers, skateboarders, young parents with baby carriages, and street musicians all dotted the streets.

"This is better than a country fair," Ginger said.

I showed the kids the terrific waterfall tucked away on Fifty-third Street. Ace said, "I bet it's just a water-main break," but I could tell he liked it. Scott squeezed my hand and whispered, "Too bad there isn't a waterfall near the gazebo. That would really be super."

As I squeezed his hand in return, I felt myself glowing. I was with this incredibly handsome boy who really wanted to be with me. We were accompanied by his sophisticated friends. They wanted me there, too. It was a dream come true. A dream I never wanted to end. The day should have been bottled so I could let out a bit of its wonder and reexperience it when I had a bad day.

We debated whether or not to visit the Museum of Modern Art. But as soon as Ginger mentioned cubist painters, Ace pretended to faint from hunger, and Scott seriously inquired if modern art included comic strips. "Probably. They have all sorts of exhibits." I entertained them with a long-winded account of a wonderful, weird, and totally imaginary show I'd gone to last spring.

I squirmed when it looked as if even Ace had been persuaded to visit the museum, which I'd never set foot in in my life. I was relieved when he said, "Nah, those crazy paintings would spoil my appetite. Wouldn't they, Nina? Tell the truth."

I gulped at his last sentence, and Scott asked if there was anything wrong. I shook my head. "We should get to the restaurant."

The Chinese restaurant was half-filled. "This is a beautiful place," Ginger said. "Look at the mural! I love those trees and birds."

The restaurant was terribly romantic. When Timothy and Zelda had taken me there, I imagined how super it would be to sit on one of the rich leather banquettes and have a good-looking boy seated across from me. We would discuss meaningful subjects while he looked deep into my eyes, thinking I was the only girl in the world for him.

The meaningful topics we now discussed were school, hockey, Wendie's party ("You're going with me, of course, Nina"), and the menu. Scott did stare deep into my eyes, though.

We ordered several dishes to share. I think the waiters and other patrons were amazed that four teenagers could be so adult. I felt older and sort of cultured—almost like a real Daltonite.

"It was perfect, wasn't it?" Scott asked as we drove back to New Jersey. We sat in the backseat, hugging each other and exchanging sweet, gentle kisses.

"Absolutely. Did you see the yachts on the river? I'd love to travel on one some evening and have a candlelight dinner." That was something I never expected to say to a boy without having him crack up or make rude noises. But then, Scott wasn't like most boys.

He kissed me several times as he walked me to the door. He wouldn't come in because Ace and Ginger were waiting, but he said, "Don't forget. Tuesday afternoon, we're going shopping for Wendie's gift."

"Oh, Wendie!" I slid the shawl off. "I almost forgot. This belongs to her. Will you take it back to the car?"

"Sure. I'm glad you're absentminded. It gives me another chance to kiss you good night." And he did, and I melted. He pulled away, and through the porch light, I could see him give me a slow, sexy smile.

Watching the car leave, I hugged myself. Scott cared about me! And I'd made a good impression on Ginger and Ace. I was sure of it. I'd have my opportunity to get the approval of the others at Wendie's party Saturday night. I could hardly wait!

Mom and Dad were watching an old movie on TV. "Have a nice time?" Mom asked.

"Wonderful." I sighed. "And it's not going to stop. Tuesday, Scott and I are going to pick out a gift for Wendie. Thursday, Ginger's coming over with her makeup kit so we can try out some stuff for the party." She'd told me so in the ladies' room of the restaurant. She said she always experimented before a big night. "Otherwise," she had said, "I'd end up looking like an entire cosmetics counter. I just want a natural look, and that takes practice."

"Earth to Nina!" Mom's voice interrupted me. "I said you're going to have a busy week."

"Yeah, I sure am."

"Topped off by sitting at Tim and Zelda's on their anniversary."

"Baby-sitting? I'm not doing that this week—"

"Of course you are," Dad said. "You always sit for them on their anniversary. You love it. A night in the penthouse, entertaining the twins, full access to the video games, the billiard—"

"Not *this* Saturday night!" I wailed.

"Yes. Nina, what's wrong?" Mom asked.

"I can't make it. I have plans! Wendie's party."

"Nina, you promised Tim and Zelda months ago. They're counting on you. They have reservations at an expensive restaurant and tickets for an impossible-to-get-tickets-for Broadway show. You know that."

The trouble was, I did know. But I'd really forgotten about the sitting job. I couldn't attend Wendie's party. My first party with Scott and the Daltonites, and I couldn't go. I dashed upstairs before Mom and Dad could see me cry.

Chapter Nine

"How am I going to tell them I can't make it?" I asked Peggy as we walked to school the following day. Jack flanked her right side; I was on the left.

"Straight out," she said, fingering the collar of her pea jacket. "Gosh. It's cold. Yesterday must have been a mirage."

"Yesterday was great," Jack put in. "Peg, Louise, Bobby, and I went over to Maitland Park and played Frisbee with Louise's Labrador. It was lots of fun."

Yesterday. My perfect day.

"It's only one party, Nina. Scott won't care."

How could Peggy be so unfeeling? What if she had to turn Jack down for the biggest party of the season? Oh, who was I kidding? She wouldn't mind missing out on a bash.

"You're still not comfortable with them."

I looked at Peg, then at Jack. He grinned.

"Girl talk. I'll leave." He walked a few feet ahead of us, where he met up with some of his friends.

Peggy and I stopped walking. "Answer my question, Nina. I've never seen you so quiet. If this is what comes from hanging out with the Daltonites, I'm glad I'm not with them. Imagine being intimidated by a bunch of flashy kids!"

"Why do you always put them down? They're nice!" I said staunchly, but I wasn't entirely sure I believed what I was saying.

"If they're so nice, why do you worry about them all the time?" Peggy asked, voicing my own fears. "Honestly, I don't get it. I can see your being worried about Scott. He's your first real boyfriend, and I know how important it is to get along with him." She nodded in Jack's direction. "I was nervous about everything when we first started going together, but now I'm relaxed."

"I'm relaxed around Scott. Pretty much so."

"Then why are you uneasy about his friends?"

How could I explain Daisy's aloofness? How I thought a wrong step with her could possibly turn the others—especially Scott—against me? How I really didn't know Marty, Duane, Wendie, or the others except for Ginger and

Ace. It was too complicated. I settled for, "They're close-knit, Peg. I want to fit in because they're important to Scott. He means everything to me. That's why this party means all it does."

"I'm sorry I came on so strong, Nina. It's just that things are changing rapidly. Your best friend is having trouble adjusting, too. I miss you. Listen, why don't you come to the library with me this afternoon?"

"Terrific. I'd like that."

Minutes later I was at my locker, fiddling with the stubborn lock, when Ginger arrived. "I can't go to the party," I blurted out before she could say hello.

"You can't? You didn't mention it yesterday."

I thought quickly before the bell rang. "I didn't know until last night. See my aunt and uncle—well, you know I baby-sit for them. I don't get paid much. Family and all. Anyhow, they like to repay me in grand style. So, Saturday night we're going to Lutece," I said, coming up with the fanciest restaurant I'd ever heard of. "And then to . . ." I dropped the name of the play Tim and Zelda were going to. "And it wouldn't be fair to turn them down after they went to all that trouble. My aunt is even buying a silk dress to wear."

Ginger's eyes widened. "That sounds fantastic! You're so lucky, Nina. We'll miss you at the party, though. I bet Scott was really disappointed."

"I—I haven't told him yet."

"You're kidding?"

"No, I mean I would've told him first thing," I said, realizing that, of course, Scott should have known before anyone else. "But he had an early practice, and I didn't want to disturb him with a call last night."

"Oh, yeah."

The bell chimed. "See you later! Gotta go!"

Whew! My little white lie had worked. I'd have to tell Scott at lunch.

As soon as I saw Scott enter the cafeteria, I joined him in the lunch line. "I have something to tell you."

"What's wrong, Nina?"

His genuine concern gave me courage. Hurriedly I filled him in on the story I'd given Ginger, careful not to embellish the supposed evening any more than I already had.

"Boy, that's a relief!" He didn't look the least bit upset!

"We wouldn't have had much fun, anyway," he said as he paid for his lunch. "I have a game Saturday afternoon and another on Sunday. My mind wouldn't have been on the party. I'd be bushed, too. I was hating the thought of spoiling the evening for you by being too exhausted to dance and then cutting out early."

I giggled. He smiled. Things were looking up!

I was in a terrific mood when I met Peg after school. Louise Chang was with her. We talked nonstop as we walked to the library. Peg found the books she needed pretty quickly, with some help from my mother. Then Peg, Louise, and I decided to go to Burger Bit for shakes. En route, we ran into Bobby and Jack. And we never stopped talking.

My old friends were great. I hadn't meant to neglect them. And I decided I wouldn't in the future. I was *so* comfortable with them! I didn't have to worry about entertaining them. And even though our class schedules differed, we still had a lot in common.

Louise sipped her shake. "My brother's covering the hockey games for the school paper." Her dark eyes twinkled. "It seems that Lincoln High has a genuine superstar in the making. Would Nina know anything about him?"

I blushed. "Mmm, a little."

"Scott Holbrook is gorgeous!" Louise said

enthusiastically. "Half the sophomore class swoons when he walks down the hall."

"I don't swoon," Bobby said solemnly.

"You're the other half." Peg laughed.

"Are you going to the games this weekend?" Louise asked.

"Only the one on Sunday. I can't make the Saturday afternoon one because—um, I have to go into the city. Come to think of it, I don't know if all the Daltonites will attend, either. They have a big party Saturday night."

"Daltonites?" came Jack's sleepy voice. He hadn't said much. He never did.

"That's what they call themselves," I said, folding a straw wrapper in thirds.

"I know," Jack said thoughtfully. "I just never really connected Scott with the Daltonites and the shore. My cousin Mary used to date one of them—not for long, though."

"Why'd they break up?" Louise wanted to know.

For some reason, the answer wasn't one I wanted to hear. The shake had left a chalky aftertaste in my mouth.

"Because it was too much for him to drive back and forth to Maitland. The shore is pretty far off."

"There are buses," Peggy said.

Jack shrugged. I closed my eyes and tried

to block out the new worry. But I couldn't. Opening my eyes, I glanced at the Burger Bit parking lot. A Daltonite had broken up with Jack's cousin because it was too much for him to drive back and forth. Scott didn't drive yet. He relied on the others. *I* relied on them, too, and the buses. What about when the bad weather came? How would Scott and I see each other? Would he be like the Daltonite Jack's cousin Mary had dated and break up with me? *No!* I wouldn't let that happen.

Chapter Ten

On the following Tuesday Ms. Perez asked me to remain after class. Scott waited for me outside the rear door; we were going to buy Wendie's gift. Ms. Perez brought up the subjects of the Thanksgiving assembly and the debate society.

"Ms. Perez, if it's not mandatory," I said slowly, "I'd rather not do it. There are so many things going on in my life right now." I cast a quick glance over my shoulder.

"It's not mandatory, Nina, and I do understand about other activities." She smiled. "But give it some thought."

I said I would, but my mind was already made up. Nothing could interfere with my new social life.

Scott and I walked to the mall five blocks from Lincoln High. He had no idea what to get Wendie, but I had a present in mind. I took him to the needlecraft section of one of the department stores. "Yarn? Needles?" he asked, puzzled, running his fingers through his thick black hair. "Wouldn't it be easier to just buy her a hat or a scarf?"

I laughed, as did the saleswoman in the needlecraft department. "Wendie loves to crochet," I said. "I bet she'd love a basket of yarns, needles, and patterns."

Scott sighed. "If you say so. I would've bought her a box of stationery. I always buy stationery for girls. Not *girlfriends*." He emphasized the difference. "They get special gifts."

"Our perfume department is on the opposite end of this floor," the saleswoman offered.

We all laughed. It was great being with Scott! Maybe I was silly about his friends. *He* liked me the way I was. Perhaps I should cut down on my exaggerations, but somehow, deep inside, I knew stopping those stories wouldn't be simple.

Since I wasn't attending the party, Ginger canceled the makeup marathon. "We'll have plenty of other opportunities," she said. "We love to throw parties."

The collective "we" again. What if *I* threw a party? It was worth thinking about. I'd invite

Peggy, Jack, Louise, and Bobby, naturally, and the Daltonites—again, naturally! I had a whole guest list written out before I even asked my parents if it'd be OK.

I nearly approached them about it on Thursday night, but two things stopped me. One, I failed an algebra test. I had to have the fifty-nine percent exam signed. I couldn't say, "Here's my flunked paper. By the way, I'd like to throw a party." Even my super-understanding parents would balk at that.

The second thing was Rory O'Toole. He was over for another tutoring session. My father had to take a call from a fellow faculty member, and Mom was in her study, working on the final draft of a fantasy story—so, I was left with Rory and the refrigerator.

"You have something good in there, kid?"

"Ice. Eggs."

"Cute, cute. C'mon, Muppet, I'm a growing boy." He flashed a phony smile. "You know how it is with us hockey players. You're seeing some jock dude, aren't you? Your old man mentioned it."

"Yes," I replied, knowing full well he'd just said that so I'd feel pleased enough to find something for him in the refrigerator.

He beamed when I pulled out Jell-O laced with pears and a platter of cheddar wedges. I handed him a spoon and a loaf of rye. He could make his own sandwich; he hadn't made me feel *that* pleased.

"Scott's probably going to be the first sophomore captain of the hockey team," I said. "I'm very proud of him. We all are."

"We? Your folks?"

"The gang. The kids from the shore."

He gulped his food, then whistled. "Daltonites, huh? They're still the ringleaders. Always were. They sure don't like outsiders."

"They don't?"

He took a long gulp of the root beer I'd also set out for him. "Nah. Hard to break through to them. You have to keep them entertained." He didn't notice my slow intake of breath. "Me, they accepted straight off because I was a superstar but anyone else, two chances of acceptance—slim and none. Hey, you a cheerleader?"

"I beg your pardon?"

" 'I beg your pardon.' Man, can you tell you're your old man's daughter! Nobody under forty says that. The Daltonites sure don't. Look, Muppet, I asked if you were a cheerleader. Pom-pom girls and the homecoming queen *might* get through the barrier. Even if this dude digs you, his friends have a lot of influence with him. No offense, kid, but you're not exactly homecoming queen material." He chuckled. "If you were, I'd ask you out myself."

"You're too old for her." Dad's voice filled the kitchen. Rory had the decency to look apologetic, but I'm sure he wasn't. It didn't matter. He'd made a valid point. The Daltonites hadn't changed since the time he'd been in Lincoln. Could Scott be swayed away from me if the others found fault with me? A horrible thought. Add that to the geographical problem. Scott meant too much to me. I couldn't let him get away from me. I'd have to make certain the kids thought I was the most entertaining person around—no matter what tales I had to invent!

"Then we had artichokes vinaigrette and mussels in cream," I ticked off the supposed menu to Ginger and the others between the first and second periods of Sunday's hockey match. We were winning two to zero on goals made by Scott. When he scored the second, he looked in the direction of our section and waved his stick.

I had no idea if Lutece served those dishes. I'd found them in one of Zelda's many cookbooks and memorized the fanciest-sounding ones. And hoped the kids never went to the restaurant.

The kids were impressed.

I was relieved. For the time being.

We won the game six to zero. I waited for Scott. After he'd showered and dressed, we went to Sal's. A huge cheer exploded when we entered. Sal was thrilled with the unexpected Sunday business, and when he discovered Scott had been the game's hero, he treated him "and his cute girl" to free soft drinks. I liked the attention, and Scott positively *loved* it. He was proud of his hockey exploits and was all caught up in them. He didn't forget me, though. From time to time he would look deep into my eyes, and I would melt.

However, reality set in as soon as we sat down. Wendie's party was Topic A. I took some comfort in something Ginger had told me earlier. "Scott missed you like crazy. He gave Wendie her gift, danced once with each girl, just to be polite, then split. Such a lost lamb!"

"You missed one super bash." Daisy's voice interrupted my thoughts. "We Daltonites really know how to throw a party!" A chorus of "Yeahs!"

"We Daltonites." I still wasn't included. At least not by Daisy. That had to change!

"I'm going to have a party," I said.

"You are?" Ace asked. "Wow! More free food!"

While everyone laughed, Scott spoke quietly. "You didn't say anything about it to me." Was there hurt in his voice?

"I didn't say anything because I wasn't positive until yesterday. My parents felt terrible that I couldn't make Wendie's party . . ." My voice trailed off. I'd almost said because I'd been baby-sitting! "So when I suggested a party, they were enthusiastic."

"When is the party?" Daisy asked.

"That's still a bit up in the air. My parents do a lot of entertaining, and we have to make sure our activities don't clash." That sounded pretty good, I thought, but the kids would want a definite date. "It'll probably be this Saturday."

"Great!" said Ginger. And *my* upcoming party became Topic A.

I wondered what my parents would say.

They were watching a late-afternoon football game when Scott dropped me off. We stood in the hall, kissing and talking. Ace's car was in the drive. "I was wondering about this party," Scott said between kisses. "Um, will you invite Rory O'Toole?"

Of all the things in the world to say. Rory at a high-school party. Ha! He'd collapse into hysterics at the very idea. But one glance at Scott's serious gray eyes told me not to say anything. I stood on tiptoe and kissed Scott's nose. "Of course Rory's invited! He wants to meet you as much as you want to meet him!"

"Wow!" Scott said, obviously impressed. We kissed again. Then Ace's horn sounded. I waved as they pulled out of the driveway. When I walked into the living room, Dad said there was cream cheese and fresh date nut bread in the refrigerator. As delicious as it sounded, I was stuffed from pizza. Besides, I wanted to call Peggy.

After informing her that Lincoln High had won and Scott had scored a hat trick, I plunged into the news of the party. She seemed hesitant at first, but when I told her I intended to invite Bobby and Louise, and whoever they wanted to bring, her interest grew.

"This Saturday night then?" she asked.

"Well, I hope so. See, I haven't exactly gotten the OK from my parents."

"Nina! You're impossible!" Peggy laughed. "Lotsa luck."

"I have a feeling I'll need it."

Fortunately the Giants held a twenty-one to six halftime lead over the Dallas Cowboys when I came downstairs. "I want to throw a party," I announced. "I'll pay for it, clean up, the whole works. I'd like it this Saturday night."

" 'Hello, Mom. Hello, Dad.' Isn't that a more customary greeting?" Dad asked, a twinkle in his eye.

"A party? Saturday night? Here? Teenagers?" Mom asked.

"No, I thought I'd invite the Maitland Nursery School." They laughed. Confidence oozed. "I have promised to pick up my algebra grade." They'd signed the failed test. "And I will." I looked expectantly at Mom.

"It's OK with me. We've met some of the kids, and we like them. And you did miss that party last night. What do you think?" she asked, nudging Dad.

He sighed and stared at the tube as the Giants lined up to receive the second-half kickoff. "Just remind me to rummage through the attic."

"The attic?" Mom and I said in unison.

"My earmuffs are up there. Look! He's running back the kickoff!"

While my parents cheered and yelled, I flopped into a wing chair, feet dangling over the side. The party would be my moment in the sun. My crowning success with the Daltonites.

Little did I dream it would be the beginning of the end.

Chapter Eleven

Bits of trouble occurred right away. Scott asked if Rory had accepted my invitation. Quickly I told him that the Parkhurst College squad had a game that night. Since they played almost every Saturday night, I figured I was covered.

In algebra I was talking to Audrey when Daisy made one of her entrances.

"Nina, you would not believe the divine outfit I got for your party! It's slinky and fits like a second skin. Wait until you see it Saturday!" She waltzed to her seat.

Audrey's lips tightened. I was in for it. "The party's a last-minute thing," I said quickly. "I was just about to invite you. You can bring a date."

Audrey shrugged. "I guess so."

Her attitude puzzled me. I thought she'd leap at the invitation. I could never figure her out. Maybe that was why we'd never been friends.

Peggy wasn't crazy about her, either. "I get the feeling that inside her chubby body is another catty Daisy Clements clawing to get out," she'd once said.

I should've listened to Peggy.

Mom loosened the purse strings on the fund so I could buy something "suitable for the hostess" to wear. I also had to buy—from my savings—place mats, paper plates, plastic cups, and streamers. I asked Peggy to go with me to the mall after school. It had been forever since we'd gone on a shopping spree together.

Peggy found a crepe blouse in deep plum and a gray wool skirt. Then I spotted a knit dress that Peggy said was perfect. I knew it was, too. When we finished with the clothes, we headed for the jewelry counter.

"Oh," Peggy cried longingly. "Those little gold earrings are gorgeous."

"They're only fifteen dollars," I said.

"Only?" Peggy grimaced.

I braced myself for the "Those kids are really influencing you, aren't they?" remark, but it never came. Peg just stared at the earrings.

"How much do you have?" I asked.

"Ten."

"I'll make up the difference."

"Nina, I couldn't let you—"

"Of course you could! The dress was really inexpensive, and I got all this party stuff on sale."

Peggy shook her head stubbornly.

"Consider it an early Christmas present. I'd probably buy earrings for you, anyhow. Who could ever forget the day we went to get our ears pierced? You were so brave! But me—I saw the guy stick pins in your lobes, and I fell out the door, and you found me cringing behind Big Bird in the toy shop. Remember?"

Peg smiled and rolled her eyes. "What an exaggeration! You weren't in the toy store. Just outside the jewelry store. On your knees and a little green, maybe." Peggy hugged me. "Thanks, Nina. You're a crazy person sometimes, but you are special."

I really felt special the night of my party. Ginger had come by early to help with preparations and my makeup. Mom said it was OK to clog my pores for one night. When Ginger was finished, I peered in the mirror. "Wow, is that dramatic!"

"Is it ever! Not something to wear to Lincoln High."

"Daisy does," I said quietly.

"Daisy is Daisy. You should know that by now."

"But you always defend her."

"Daisy's had it rough."

"She has?" I asked, genuinely surprised.

"She won't admit it. Her parents split up years ago. She lives with her father. He's never remarried. He's the owner of Clements Manufacturing."

"He is? I always see their commercials on the local stations. I think Uncle Timothy handled that account."

Ginger adjusted the clasp on her necklace. "Mr. Clements is the president of the company, but he really doesn't do anything. The place runs itself. He checks in at the office a couple of times a week, and that's it. The rest of the time he has nothing to do."

"Does he spend a lot of time with Daisy then?"

"That's just it, Nina, he doesn't. My mother says he's still carrying a torch for his ex-wife. She lives in California and hardly ever gets in touch with them. Mr. Clements doesn't know what to do with a teenaged daughter, especially one as difficult as Daisy. So Daisy really needs her friends, Wendie in particular. Wendie's so stable."

So, I understood Daisy Clements a little better. I wondered how envious of the Daltonites Peggy would be if she knew Daisy's story. The Blairs might've had a financial setback, but the family was still together. Well, I wasn't going to dwell on depressing subjects. It was my party, and I was going to enjoy it!

It started off just fine.

Everyone looked terrific and was in high spirits. Daisy breezed in with Chuck Vanci. I gazed hurriedly at Bobby. Had he seen? Vividly I recalled my conversation with Bobby the day I'd handed him his invitation.

"Daisy Clements will be there, won't she, Nina?" he asked excitedly.

"All the Daltonites will. Um, do you like Daisy?" I tried to sound nonchalant.

"What guy wouldn't? She's a knockout! I know she comes on a little strong, but I think underneath she's probably pretty vulnerable." He blushed. "I think she kind of likes me. Kind of."

"Oh, Daisy is an incurable flirt!" I waved my hand. "She flirts with all the guys. But she would never, ever date a boy who wasn't from the shore. She has a crazy rule about that."

Bobby looked depressed. I really didn't want to study his face when Daisy walked in with Chuck. Chuck lives three houses down from me. Not exactly a Daltonite. Would Bobby comment on that? It was just my first worry of that long night.

"Everything looks fantastic," Scott said, placing an arm around my shoulders and drawing me to him.

"Thanks," I said, forgetting about Bobby. My parents and I had moved all the furniture into the dining room and had pulled up the rugs. My father had hung the streamers while Mom had dragged out the utility table. I had put out the refreshments and set up the stereo speakers on the mantel and in the bay window. My parents had warned the neighbors I'd be having a party, which would end by one.

During the evening my parents stayed in their bedroom mostly, making infrequent and inconspicuous visits to the party. Once I saw Mom talking with Ace. From the gleam in their eyes and the incredulous look on Ginger's face, I gathered they were discussing Mom's latest sale.

The party had been going on for about an hour when the second incident occurred. With the music blasting, I didn't hear the phone.

Mom called me into her den. I stepped over the books and shut the door. Who would be phoning during the party? All my friends were here.

"I'm not coming. If you haven't guessed that already," someone said curtly.

"Audrey, is that you?"

"Didn't you even notice I hadn't shown up?"

I bit my lip. "Oh, I thought you might be late. Not everyone shows up on time. Some people think it's fashionable to be late." How glib I'd become lately!

"That's not a very good pun, Nina."

"Audrey, I don't know what you're talking about. I didn't make any pun—"

" 'Fashionable.' You would say that to me, wouldn't you? I bet you and your snobby group get lots of laughs at my expense."

I stared at the receiver. What was she carrying on about?

"You weren't going to invite me, were you, Nina? You only did because Daisy Clements mentioned it in front of me, and you were too embarrassed to say anything else."

"That's not true!"

"True? What would you know about truth, Nina Ward?"

My stomach turned, and I tried to convince

myself it was from the chili dog and banana ice cream I'd eaten. But Audrey went on.

"Daisy told me she'd like to come to one of my Lane Bryant shows. 'Nina told us all about it. Chubby is in and all,' she said. Then how you 'helped' me with my performance and how I needed you for moral support."

I sat on the edge of Mom's cluttered desk. I was glad she'd left me alone to take the call. I knew I had probably turned beet red.

"You never went with me to Lane Bryant."

"Did—did you tell Daisy that?" I asked.

I could almost see her smirking. "Not yet."

And the phone clicked. I stared at the receiver. No! Audrey wouldn't tell Daisy! Or would she? What would happen then? How could I get out of this situation? My mind was already flying, trying to think of stories that would remedy the uncomfortable situation. But no tales popped into my head. The door opened; I jumped.

"I'm sorry. I knocked twice."

"Peg, it's you! Thank goodness!"

"Nina, what's wrong? You look worried. Is it the phone call?"

"No. It was Audrey. She's not coming."

"She picked a fine time to tell you. She's kind of peculiar sometimes."

I wanted to get off the subject. "Did you want to ask me something?"

"Scott and Jack are discussing goalie averages. I never realized Jack was such a hockey fanatic. We're going to the next game with all of you."

Instantly Audrey was pushed to the back of my mind. Peggy's face glowed. She grabbed my hand. "I'm sorry about the Daltonite cracks I made. They *are* a good bunch. Ace Turner asked me to dance and said I reminded him of this enchantress he'd read about once. Then he launched into a detailed summary of the book. He was so much fun." She shook her head. "When the dance was over, he took me over to Ginger, and we got to talking, and Jack came over and—it was just super. *They're* super."

"I told you they were nice."

"I know." She shrugged. "I think maybe, just maybe—no, definitely—I was jealous of them. With all their money and stuff. Or maybe we've just been reading them wrong all this time. Maybe we believed they wouldn't let in outsiders, so they just acted that way. I don't know. The only one I still can't figure out is Daisy. But anyway, I take back some of what I said before."

That took courage! I felt a lot better. Until we stepped into the kitchen.

My appetite had returned. Marty, Wendie, and Duane were already there.

"I have an insatiable appetite for rocky road ice cream," Wendie said sheepishly.

"Since you and Marty brought all the Baskin-Robbins, you're each entitled to as much as you want," I said. "Thanks for bringing it. That was really nice."

The music stopped. One of the kids popped in another cassette. In seconds the Stones came blaring on.

"You two really had a wild time at that concert, didn't you?" Marty asked.

Peggy smiled. "Yeah, it was wild. The Garden was really rocking."

"Not the concert itself. Afterward," Marty said. "When you two went to that dope party in SoHo and got lost coming back—"

"And then you had to sneak into your house," Wendie said.

I wanted to die. I mean, at that moment I think I honestly wished I were not alive.

Duane spoke. "Then your fat cat wouldn't budge from the window."

Peggy hates to have Damien called fat. The three Daltonites were still grinning when they left the kitchen.

"Nina, how could you?"

"You just told me you liked the kids."

"I'm not talking about them, and you know it! What dope party? We never went anywhere after the concert. And we certainly didn't sneak into my house, and my 'fat' cat did not block a window. What kind of crazy story did you make up?"

"Just one of my usual crazy stories," I said as blithely as I could with chili dog and banana ice cream once again rising in my throat. "You love my stories. They do, too. It was just a harmless tale."

"I don't care what they loved! I don't appreciate a starring role in one of your imagined adventures. From now on, keep me out of your creative efforts!" Peggy started to storm out, then stopped. For a second, relief swept over me. She'd flown off the handle. She did that a lot. Now she was over it.

"That's how you did it, didn't you?"

"Did what?" I asked.

"Got them to like you so quickly. You made up stories to entertain them." Audrey popped to the front of my mind again.

"Just a few."

"Well, let me tell you something. Those weren't just stories; they were lies. Nina, how could you?" She fled from the kitchen.

How could I? It'd been so easy. Too easy. Now the stories were catching up with me. I thought of Audrey and her "not yet" remark. A chill ran through me. How many of my half-truths would be found out?

Chapter Twelve

Ms. Perez expressed disappointment when I refused to join the debate society or take part in the Thanksgiving-week assembly. "You have such a natural gift for communicating, Nina. Do you have an after-school job or brothers and sisters to take care of?"

I sat beside her desk. Snow swirled outside as the Daltonites hurried to their bus. I would have to walk home alone. Peggy had been cool to me since the party; Audrey wouldn't even look at me; even friendly Bobby was aloof. I tried to convince myself that it didn't matter. So what if my old friends stayed away? The group liked me—more than ever. The party had been a huge success, even if for me, the evening still remained a blur. Scott was sweet and attentive, as usual, but for a million dollars, I couldn't remember anything he'd said. My memories were only of Audrey's call, Bobby's hurt face when Daisy strolled in with Chuck, and Peggy's anger. I couldn't convince myself that my old friends didn't matter. They did. A lot. And a nagging voice told me to watch my step with the new ones, too.

"I don't have an after-school job or anyone to care for, Ms. Perez, but I do have a whole group of new friends, and they don't live in Maitland, so when I go out with them, there's a lot of travel involved and—" I shrugged. "There's a boy, too. A special one."

She nodded sympathetically. "But Scott—yes, teachers are aware of what's going on among their students—has hockey. He's *very* involved with that. Surely he wouldn't mind if you spent time on other activities."

"Oh, no. He'd encourage—"

"I thought so. He seems to be a very sensible young man. There's something else troubling you, Nina. Would you like to tell me about it?"

I declined her kind invitation.

Outside the thick snow encircled me. I wondered how long it would take the bus to reach the shore. My waterproof boots thumped the ground, snow blinding me. I bumped into an inanimate object. At least I thought it was inanimate until it gave a loud "Ouch!"

"Sorry. I can't see a thing."

"Is that another lie? Why can't you just admit you're a klutz, Nina? Or don't your precious Daltonites approve of klutzes? At least, I'm not one. As chubby as I am, I'm graceful." And with that, Audrey stomped away.

I realized begging her not to tell the gang I'd fudged a little on reality wouldn't do a bit of good. If she was determined to tell them, she would. I had to be prepared. How? I still hadn't come up with anything. Possibly because a part of me yearned to stop telling . . . lies. That's what I was beginning to see them as. They were habit forming. Like cigarettes? Maybe I could ask Dad how it was when he stopped smoking.

He was in his study, just lighting his pipe when I barged in. "The abominable snowperson." He sighed. "That's some storm, isn't it? How about some hot chocolate and cranberry bread?" He glanced longingly at his pipe. "You and your mom have built-in radar. You instinctively know when I'm going to light up."

"The bread and cocoa sound super. Let me just take off my wet things first."

When I entered the kitchen, the hot chocolate was steaming, and Dad had cut large wedges of moist cranberry bread for us.

"I have a serious question to ask you," I said.

"Maybe I should pour myself a double?" He gestured to the steaming pot. I was too upset to laugh.

"I want to ask about your smoking."

He sat across from me, his green eyes full of concern. "Nina, you haven't started smoking?"

"No!"

"That's a relief. What then?"

"What was it like when you stopped? You went cold turkey. How did you feel? Emotionally I mean."

He was silent for a moment, then said, "It wasn't easy. I got cravings for cigarettes all the time. I wondered what was wrong with me. I tried more than once, you know—"

"You did? You never told Mom or me—"

"I didn't want to disappoint anyone. I'll admit the first efforts were halfhearted. I kept telling myself I could give them up anytime I wanted to. Then I realized I couldn't. That made me angry. And that's when I announced to you I was going cold turkey."

"So then how'd you feel?"

"Like a freak of nature. I'd heard all these stories about people who'd quit and how they'd gotten their sense of taste back, could jog, lost their hacking cough. And there I was, dying for a smoke most of the time. I constantly fought the urge to plunk coins into the cigarette machine in the faculty lounge."

"Really? You never mentioned that before."

"It was embarrassing. You and your mother were so proud of me that I couldn't very well admit I'd nearly slipped up."

"How did you know when you were cured?"

His answer shocked me. "I'm still not. Why do you think I smoke the pipe? I'm trying to stop that, too. Have you ever noticed I'm always just lighting up when someone walks in?" I nodded. "It's because I hear the car in the drive or the door slam, and I know someone's about to stop me. It's childish, but grown-ups, as you know by now, Nina, are not perfect beings. Have I answered your question?"

"Yes," I said, chewing a piece of cranberry bread.

"Why do I get the feeling your mind is elsewhere? You asked about my smoking in reference to something else, didn't you?"

"Yeah. But I can't talk about it. Don't be upset. It's nothing serious." Just my whole life, my new-found popularity, and my boyfriend were at stake.

"Whenever you want to talk about it, let me know. Meanwhile, I have some news that'll cheer you up. It's about Rory."

"He's finally passing English lit, and he'll never darken our doorway or hog our front hall mirror again?"

"Not quite," Dad said, chuckling. "It seems that Rory will be at the Lincoln-Tyler hockey game this weekend."

"Wow! That's our biggest one to date. We're tied for first. Scott's having extra practices because of it."

"I thought it might be an important game. But that's not the whole reason Rory's going. He played a banner game against Tyler in his senior year. He's trying to relive old memories. At his age!" Dad roared.

I thanked Dad for the info. Tomorrow, I'd tell Scott. And tomorrow, I'd also halt my lies. If my dad could give up smoking, I could certainly let go of my tale-telling. Besides, I had a true story for Scott. No need for any more fabrications!

Chapter Thirteen

"Rory O'Toole can't wait to see you play! He's making a special trip to the game. It's the first chance he's had to attend a Lincoln game. He has so many fond memories of playing against Tyler." My mouth seemed to have a mind of its own. It was the day after I had resolved not to fabricate stories.

"He had a double-hat trick against them in his senior year," Scott said. "I'd love to do that, too."

We were in the cafeteria line. He placed macaroni surprise on his tray. The surprise was whether it was defrosted. One could never be sure if the steam emanating from the little aluminum container was dry ice or warmth.

"Man, he's coming to see *me* play. I can't believe it! Thanks, Nina."

"Why are you thanking me?" I asked, paying the cashier. "I didn't do anything."

"Of course you did," Scott said. "You put in a few good words for me with Rory O'Toole. Don't be modest about it."

"Scott, I swear I didn't," I said, telling the truth for once. His deep gray eyes bore into mine. "Well, I did mention we're sort of, you know, going together—"

Scott stopped in the middle of the cafeteria. As a straw wrapper sailed past my head, he said, "We're not *sort of* going together, Nina. We *are* going together. You're my girl. Everyone knows it. Except for you sometimes."

I smiled. Now, what else could I say to Scott after he said something that wonderful? I said, "Rory is very impressed that we're a couple. He thinks you're the best hockey player at Lincoln since himself. And believe me, he has a lot of, um, confidence in his own ability."

"Athletes have to have that. I have it, too." Not the way Rory O'Toole does, I thought. Thank goodness.

Well, I couldn't help that story. Scott had practically insisted on it. OK, I could've stuck with the whole truth. Rory would attend the game. Period. No embellishments. But when Scott looked at me the way he had and said what he said about our being a couple, I couldn't very well leave the story unvarnished. Could I?

The question nagged at me through lunch. Look, Dad attempted to quit smoking several times and hadn't told anyone about his attempts. I hadn't announced, "Nina Ward is throwing in the towel on her tale-telling." So, this little white lie didn't count. Yeah. I could start over again. Right now. Or later. That reasoning made me feel better. I wondered how Ginger was feeling. She'd caught a cold in the snowstorm and was absent. Scott filled the kids in on the Rory story.

"That's super," Marty said. "I know how I'd feel if some superstar from the area came to watch me play. What a break!"

"Yeah, and I have Nina to thank for it."

"That was a great party," Ace said, as the conversation turned to me.

I smiled, and they were off on the one subject I didn't want to discuss. How could I get them off it? Duane supplied me with the perfect opening to change the subject. "I didn't realize your mother was *the* Mrs. Ward from the Maitland Library. I have to do a paper on medieval customs for world history and the shore branch doesn't have a good section. The librarian told me to ask for Mrs. Ward at Maitland. I stopped by Maitland, and there was your mother! And she was super about helping me. She knows that place inside out!"

"And the people. You should hear her talk about the regulars."

"Regulars like at a bar?" Duane asked.

"Something like that," I said. "You'd be surprised how many people hang out at libraries. It's free, warm in the winter, air-conditioned in the summer, and some people are actually addicted to books."

"What are they like?" Daisy asked.

In view of what happened next, it was ironic she'd been so curious. Deciding I could go cold turkey tomorrow, I launched into tales of the library regulars. I got to the Golfer. "My mother says he's wealthy, dresses in three-piece Brooks Brothers' suits, carries a watch fob, wears a diamond tie clasp, the whole bit. He told Mom he belongs to the country club, but he gets bored after a few rounds of golf, so he comes to the library. He raids the archaeology and divorce books. Mom thinks it's sad he can't find something more fulfilling to do with his time and energy."

There was a hush from the kids, and I hoped I hadn't said anything too heavy. Then Duane muttered, "Wow!" And Scott shook his head sympathetically. "Poor guy." I knew they'd liked the story.

Except for Daisy. She snapped, "That is the dumbest, weirdest bit of garbage I've heard you tell yet, Nina Ward! You know, sometimes I think you just make things up! Excuse me, I have to go to the bathroom!"

And she flounced away. I chewed my lip. Marty said, "Don't mind her, Nina. She gets awfully moody. I don't know how Wendie can put up with her sometimes."

Scott put his strong arm around my shoulders. It should have comforted me, but what Daisy had said caused goose bumps up and down my arms. She was right, of course. I was exaggerating. But I'd exaggerated before. Had Audrey gotten to her? No, Audrey had ignored me in algebra and oral communications. If she'd spoken to Daisy, she would've smirked or made some remark. No, something else was bothering Daisy, and it wasn't moodiness.

I phoned Ginger that night. Her head was stuffed up, and she sneezed a good deal, but she could talk. "Even if I couldn't talk I'd just listen to the latest news," she said.

I gave her the oral communications assignment and was wondering whether to mention Daisy, when she said, "What did you talk about at lunch?"

I told her. When I finished about the Golfer, she remained silent for a long time.

Finally, she spoke. "Nina, Daisy was at lunch today, wasn't she?"

"Sure—" Why was I getting goose bumps again?

"Nina, your Golfer is Mr. Clements, Daisy's father."

"Oh, no! I had no idea. No wonder she stormed out of the lunchroom."

"I'm not surprised," Ginger said, and sneezed. "You had no way of knowing. Luckily the other kids don't know about her father, either. Not the way Wendie and I do."

Which explained the reactions I'd gotten from the boys. "Too bad neither you or Wendie was at lunch to keep my mouth shut when it started moving too fast for its own good."

Ginger sneezed again. "What? Couldn't hear that last part."

"Nothing. Oh, I'm sorry about what happened. Daisy isn't crazy about me to begin with. Now she's really offended."

"Probably embarrassed, too. Listen, Nina, it'll take her a while to cool down. Steer clear of her for a few days. When she's crossed," she warned, "or thinks she's been crossed, she can get awfully nasty. But she will get over this," she assured me. "Wendie and I will talk to her. For the time being—"

"Don't worry! I'm not going near her."

Although Ginger said Daisy would get over it, I wasn't totally convinced. Daisy had never really accepted me into the Daltonites. Now she had the perfect reason for wanting to get rid of me. Could she do it? Did she have the power?

Chapter Fourteen

Ginger, who'd finally gotten over her miserable cold, attended the Lincoln-Tyler game wrapped in a down coat, a muffler, and a matching hat. "Don't I remind you of something?"

"A photo in *Vogue*?" My gray jeans and pea coat looked downright dowdy in comparison.

"No! More like those first-graders who get so bundled up by their mommies they can't move! I'm surprised Mom didn't pin my mittens to my coat!" We laughed. "Ace is still parking the car. Wendie and Daisy went for refreshments. How's *that* situation going, Nina?"

I studied the arena. We had a banner that read Hat-Trick Holbrook, but mostly, the banners were for Tyler players, since it was Tyler ice.

"Is it so awful that you don't want to answer?"

"Well, Daisy hasn't made any remarks. I followed your advice and steered clear of her, which was easier than I anticipated."

"You mean she avoided you?"

"Yeah. Do you think she's waiting for the ideal moment, and then she'll let me have it?"

"It's a distinct possibility."

"Waiting for the other shoe to drop. Like with Audrey."

"What?"

"Um, Audrey Van, the chubby model; she's a lot like that," I said hurriedly.

"Oh." As the teams glided on to the rink, Ginger said, "You know, there is another possibility. Daisy may have discussed the incident with Wendie, and Wendie told her to forgive and forget. Wendie likes you, Nina."

"That would be super. After all, I wasn't malicious. Ignorant but not malicious."

"It would explain why Daisy's stayed clear of you. She's just licking her wounds. But she'll come around. Relieved?"

"You'd better believe it!" I said, relaxing against the cold plastic seat.

"Where are Peggy and Jack? I thought Peggy said they'd come to some games."

"Oh, Jack had to work, and Peggy hates going anywhere without him." Ginger took my answer in good faith. Peggy was still being cool to me. More than cool, as a matter of fact. I'd called her twice. The first time, her mother said she was in the tub. Peg never returned the call. The second time, Peggy answered and cut me short after I asked her if she was coming to the Lincoln-Tyler game. "To find out more ridiculous stories about myself? No, thanks, Nina." I knew I shouldn't have exaggerated the Stones concert evening. But I didn't think it would hurt anyone, let alone my best friend! The story had made such a good impression with the Daltonites. That was all I'd wanted to accomplish.

The game began. What a first period it was! The action slowed a little in the second, but Lincoln scored twice. Our section went wild, and I screamed the loudest when Scott scored a short-handed goal. Unfortunately, Tyler had also put two behind the nets, so going into the third period, we were knotted.

Ginger, Wendie, Daisy—who hadn't said anything beyond a curt hi—and I were returning from the ladies' room when Daisy said, "Who is that unbelievable hunk?"

We glanced in the direction of Daisy's hot pink, pointed fingernail. I sucked in my breath. Leaning against a pillar, munching on a hot dog, was none other than Rory O'Toole.

"Oooh, he is dynamite!" Wendie said.

"He makes the boys in our school look like kindergarten refugees," Daisy said, and giggled.

"He looks familiar. I've seen him somewhere," Ginger said thoughtfully. "Doesn't he look familiar, Nina?"

The hairs on the back of my neck bristled. My throat ached for a soft drink. I croaked. "That's Rory O'Toole."

"*You* know him?" Daisy whirled around. Challenge rang in her voice.

"Oh, yeah," Ginger said. "He's the superstar from Parkhurst College. I've seen his picture in the paper."

A tall, curvaceous blond breezed past us and over to Rory. He put his arm around her tiny waist, and they walked into the auditorium. Not a flicker of recognition in Rory's eyes when he passed me.

"He sure didn't seem to know *you.*"

Again, a dare in Daisy's crisp voice. I managed a weak smile. "I don't think he wants to bother with high-school kids while he has that beautiful college girl with him."

Wendie giggled. "Nina's right. Anyway, Daisy, that guy is here to see Scott play, remember?"

What Daisy said in reply, I don't know. I just wanted to return to our seats. ". . . that guy is here to see Scott play, remember?" I didn't want to think about that particular story!

The third period went from dull to sloppy and penalty-filled, with the teams seemingly content to tie, which they did.

"What a letdown!" Duane complained when we filed out of the building.

But when Scott exited from the dressing room some twenty minutes later, no one said anything negative. All for one and one for all, I thought for the umpteenth time.

Ace said, "Great game for you." Marty complimented him on the short-handed goal. Scott stood in the middle of the narrow side street, his dark hair still damp. He gripped his hockey equipment. "Oh, come off it. We played lousy. I didn't help when I took that third-period penalty for high-sticking. We were on our own power play then. I couldn't do much from the penalty box."

We were all silent. How different Scott was from boorish Rory! Maybe that would buoy him. "Scott, the whole team had troubles, but you did the best you could. Don't get down on yourself. I'm sure Rory O'Toole was impressed with your play."

I saw a flicker of interest in Scott's tired

eyes. "Was he here? I didn't notice him in the stands."

"He's not the kind of guy you boys would notice." Daisy laughed. "We saw him by the refreshment stand, but Nina didn't introduce us. I'm surprised, since I thought they're supposed to be good friends."

Redness crept into my face. Wendie saved me. "Daisy, it may be difficult for you to grasp, but Rory's date was the only female he saw."

"I'm sure he was impressed with you," I said again, grabbing Scott's free hand.

He kissed my forehead. "Thanks, Nina. C'mon, let's go to Sal's!" Everybody cheered. Except Daisy.

As we walked to the parking lot, I wondered about her. Was something more than just the Golfer story bothering her? Daisy and I shared three classes with Audrey. Had Audrey let the other shoe drop after all?

But Daisy and Audrey combined couldn't cause the trouble I caused for myself.

Sal's was jammed, and we had to wait for tables. Finally, we got a view into the rear of the parlor. My heart stopped. Rory, his date, and another college couple were sitting at a table, sipping beers and eating pizza.

"Look, there's your friend," Daisy said, glaring at me. She smirked, and suddenly she was quite unattractive. I held onto Scott for dear life. But he couldn't protect me against myself.

"Hey, I'd like to talk to him. I mean, he did come to the game to see me."

Before I could utter a word of protest, Scott pulled me along to the back table. We stood there for a few miserable seconds as the rest of the Daltonites brought up the rear. The quartet at the table ignored us until Rory's date glanced up. "We're not through yet, kids. You'll have to wait for another table."

"Oh, we're not waiting for the table. Hi, Rory," Scott said affably, extending his hand. "Thanks for coming to see me play today."

"Who are you, kid?"

Those words seemed to boom off the walls. I didn't dare look at Scott.

"I'm Scott Holbrook," he mumbled.

"Is that supposed to mean some—? Hey, it's the Muppet!"

"The Muppet?" Duane whispered.

"He means *her*," Daisy snapped.

Scott sounded weak, and I'm sure he was redder than the tomato sauce. "I just wanted to thank you for coming to the game. We didn't play that great but . . ."

Rory hooted. "You're not kidding. Lincoln stunk! I only came to the game because you were playing Tyler. I used to cream them single-handedly." He continued bragging, but nobody was listening.

"C'mon, Scott," Ace said. "Sal's got tables for us."

"In a minute," Scott said evenly. He shook free of me. I had to meet his blazing eyes. "I thought you told me he came to see me."

"I—"

"She lies about everything, Scott. You should know that," Daisy said delightedly. "Rory coming to see you, going to that modeling show, and who knows what else."

Audrey *had* gotten to Daisy! How could she be so mean? But I wasn't angry at Audrey. Or Daisy. Just at myself.

"Scott," I whispered. "Could we leave—"

"Why should Scott leave? He hasn't done anything to be ashamed of." Marty's usually good-humored voice was filled with contempt.

I glanced frantically at Ginger, but her back was to me. On purpose? Why not? I'd done the worst thing imaginable. I'd hurt Scott, my boyfriend. Of all people.

I fled from the pizzeria. No footsteps behind me, no shouts of "Wait, Nina! I understand perfectly!" No sounds at all except the sobs in my throat.

Chapter Fifteen

My parents looked surprised when I returned from the hockey game. No car full of laughing, shouting kids was outside, no handsome boyfriend kissing me in the hallway. Just Nina, trudging home from the bus stop.

"Did you lose?" Dad asked, looking up from the newspaper.

"You could say that. Oh, the game. No, it was a tie."

"Are you OK?" Mom asked when I declined her specialty, hamburgers au gratin.

"I think I ate too much pizza."

They were perceptive enough to realize something was amiss, but they kept their distances, knowing I wanted to be alone. I buried my crying in my pillow, but some got out—heard over half of Maitland I'm sure. Eventually a dreamless sleep arrived.

When I woke up on Sunday, not even the

aroma of sausage and freshly baked french bread could perk me up. I just lay there, staring at the ceiling, wondering how I could have been so dense. The lies had been getting longer and longer. Why hadn't I stopped them? I'd wanted to several times. But I still felt I had to impress the Daltonites because they meant everything to me. Because Scott meant everything. And when I faced the problem, I realized that I didn't like myself much and was afraid they'd feel the same way.

Oh, Scott. I kept seeing him, humiliated and hurt. If only I'd never fibbed about Rory! Again, I was kidding myself. The story was but one of a hundred lies I'd told. Except that that one was the worst because it had hurt Scott. How could I have been so cruel?

When I flatly refused the bread and sausage, Mom rapped on my door. "Want to talk about it?" she asked when I said she could come in.

"I don't think it would do much good," I replied, sitting up. "You wouldn't believe how dumb I've been. You'll disown me."

Mom smoothed the edges of her ruffled robe. "I doubt that. Did you have a fight with Scott? First fights can be awful. I remember."

"I wish it were just a fight," I said, choking back sobs. "Mom, I've made an absolute fool of myself!" The tears started. Mom held me close for a minute, then handed me several tissues from the box on the desk.

"Crying is supposed to be wonderful for the emotions, but it certainly does play havoc with the face, doesn't it?"

"Oh, Mom!" I clutched her. "They hate me. I don't have any friends. They hate me. Scott hates me. *I* hate me."

"Come on, Nina. It can't be that bad. You're such a positive, imaginative person, Nina—"

"I despise my imagination!" I said fiercely. "That's what got me into this mess. If I didn't have such a huge imagination, I might have a few friends left. At least, I think I would."

"You're not making much sense, but go on," she said, giving me a quick hug. "Just give it to me straight."

I blew my nose and looked into Mom's calm face. "What is straight? I don't know anymore. I've been telling stories for so long, I can't separate what *I* mean from what others want to hear."

"You told stories to the Daltonites?"

"Right. But they were more like lies, actually."

"And to Scott?"

"Just the one about Rory O'Toole being a big fan of his."

"Nina, Rory is a fan of himself! An exclusive club!"

"I know. It seemed like a harmless story until Rory showed up at yesterday's game. I told Scott he'd be there because of Scott, which wasn't true, and Scott confronted Rory, and you know how gross Rory is—"

"Oh. In front of all the other kids?"

"Every single one of them. One of my other stories caught up with me, too. You know Audrey Van?" Mom nodded. "Well, she modeled last summer at Lane Bryant, and I said I helped her in the show. She found out about that story from Daisy Clements and set Daisy straight."

"And Daisy has never been your greatest booster."

"That is an understatement." Then I blurted out all the tales, including the one about Peggy.

"So, *that's* why she hasn't called since the party. I was wondering about that."

"I really messed up, huh?" I said, sniffling.

"Yes, I guess so."

"You didn't have to agree so quickly!" I moaned.

"I'm not about to lie to you, Nina. There's been enough of that going on lately. You lied to Ace, too, about the number of stories I sold. I was flattered by the exaggeration and realized you were only trying to impress your new friends, so I didn't say anything. Perhaps I should have," she said thoughtfully. "I had no idea what proportions your stories had taken."

"Stories shouldn't hurt people, particularly the storyteller," I grumbled. Mom cast a disapproving glance in my direction.

"Nina, were you really so awed by those kids?"

"I guess. They're a loyal, close-knit group, and if they didn't like me, I wouldn't last long with Scott. I also think maybe I wanted them to like me so I could prove to myself I was important." There. I had said it. "But mostly it was Scott."

"He strikes me as a boy with a mind of his own, not one who'd be influenced by friends," Mom said.

I nodded my head. She hugged me again. "Nina, I know it seems like the end of the world, and it will probably seem that way for a while. But it *will* blow over."

She kissed me, then handed me the box of tissues. I needed them.

I dreaded going to school on Monday. I left late, thereby avoiding Peggy and Jack. Even so, Ginger was at her locker when I got there. She'd said hello to me from the first day of school. But now, she barely nodded. At least, I think she nodded. She inclined her head, but she could have been looking at her boots. A half-formed apology died in my throat.

Lunchtime brought more pain. I had to sit alone. The Daltonites were half the cafeteria away. No one came near me. At the end of that agonizing period, Audrey stopped by. "It's all over school, you know. What do you have to say now?" She didn't wait for an answer.

I held my head as high as possible and hurried off to algebra. Ms. Burke called on me twice, and twice received no intelligent replies. To make matters worse—after I didn't know the answers—she called on Audrey and Daisy, and they gave the correct answers, with more than passing sneers in my direction.

Oral communications was the class I dreaded most, however. Oral book reports were to begin. I'd read a wonderful romantic suspense novel by Barbara Michaels, but I couldn't remember the characters or the name of the mansion or anything. Well, it didn't matter. I wouldn't volunteer today.

Ms. Perez said, "I've put all of your names in a hat, and I'll pick them out at random.

That way some of you who are reluctant to volunteer might not be able to hide until the end." Groans. She shrugged and pulled a slip of paper from the fedora. "I don't believe it!" she cried. "Nina, you're first again!"

I could say I hadn't finished the book yet. She'd lower my grade by a full point if I did that, but at least I would give a good report when she called on me again. However, I had finished the novel, and I was through with lying. So I made my way unsteadily to the front of the room. I gave the author and book title. My voice cracked. Character names and plot twists were a jumble. Ms. Perez stared at me oddly. I heard a few snickers from the Daltonites as I gulped off ends of sentences and desperately tried to recall important incidents in the book.

"It's hard sticking to the facts, huh?" Ace whispered as I rushed back to my seat.

"Quiet!" Ms. Perez ordered. "I'm not sure anyone here will give a perfect presentation."

She was being kind, but it didn't make me feel any better. I quickly glanced over at Scott knowing full well he'd never look my way again. How could I have hurt him so much? He hadn't deserved it. If only I could explain. If only he would listen.

When oral communications blessedly ended,

Ms. Perez gestured for me to stay after class. She didn't hesitate. "What happened, Nina?" she asked. "I know you can do better than that." Then more softly she added, "There's something bothering you. I can tell." Meaning she'd noticed I'd become an outcast.

"A lot's bothering me, Ms. Perez. But I shouldn't have let it mess up the report. I really enjoyed the book."

"All right, Nina." She sighed. "I hope you can work things out. You can always talk to me, you know."

I nodded, not believing anything would ever get straightened out. Especially not when I ran into Bobby Danbury outside the building.

"You were wrong," he said without preface.

"So what else is new?" Then I looked at his face. It was smiling. "What are you talking about?"

"Daisy Clements does date boys from Maitland."

"Like Chuck. I know. I'm sorry, Bobby. I shouldn't have interfered—"

"You shouldn't have," he said amicably, "but you did. You figured someone as flashy as Daisy might end up hurting me."

"That's true."

"You went about it all wrong."

"That's also true," I said on a sigh.

We fell into step together. "I asked her out, and she said yes. We're going to the hockey game Friday."

The first game I wouldn't attend.

"I had asked her out for Saturday originally, but she's going to a big party."

Ginger's birthday party. I still had the engraved vellum invitation on my desk. Should I RSVP? Who would care?

We reached my block. "I'm glad you ignored me and asked Daisy out."

"So am I," he said, laughing. "Face it, I have to make my own decisions." He waved and crossed the street.

Decisions. I had a few of those to make myself.

Chapter Sixteen

Peggy was astonished to find me sitting on her enclosed porch, algebra text on my lap. "Actually, I'm not doing the homework. I'm too worried about what to say to you to concentrate on anything." Stopping at Peg's, instead of going to my house, was my first decision.

"Since when do you have to worry about what to say?" Peggy asked, putting her key in the door. She didn't actually invite me inside, but she kept the door open, so I followed her.

"You haven't remarked that you're dumbfounded I had the unmitigated gall to show up."

She put her books on the hall table and petted Damien, who was perched on it. "Nina, I am utterly shocked that you showed up on my doorstep—shocked that it took you so long!"

We hugged, and I cried. Peggy led me over to the lumpy blue couch. Damien purred at my ankles, then leaped on the sofa and pushed against my chin. With the long, silky angora fur tickling me, I couldn't cry anymore. I giggled. I started talking. "I'm sorry for embarrassing you, Peggy, and for acting like such a jerk. I never dreamed my stories—lies, I'm calling them what they really are—could hurt people."

"Nina, the more I thought about the story you'd made up about the concert, the less angry I became. In fact, I began to wish all those weird things had happened!"

"You're kidding?" I gulped.

"No. See, when Marty, Duane, and Wendie mentioned that story, I thought the Daltonites were having a grand old time laughing behind my back. Then I realized they weren't." She paused and removed her coat. I did the same. "They were sort of envious, which was funny, because I'd been jealous of them. I got to thinking, 'Hey, you were worried what those kids thought of you!' That's when I saw what *you* must have been going through, wanting to get tight with them."

"You saw that?" I was the one who was shocked now.

"Yeah. They're an elite clique. I told you

from the beginning they seem to have their own way of thinking, joking, dressing, et cetera. They can make a newcomer feel like an invader from Ork." She smiled. "When I considered that, I realized you weren't being malicious with your story—"

"Thoughtless, though. I only considered my feelings, my obsession with getting in with the Daltonites. I never considered the feelings of the others who appeared in my sto—lies. It was stupid." I petted Damien. "And I'm paying the price."

Softly Peggy said, "It's all over the sophomore class about you and Scott breaking up."

"I figured. The whole group broke up with me, you know."

"Those lies. They caught up with you?"

"I'll say."

Peggy didn't ask for specifics. She understood I was hurting. "Can I help?"

"You'd want to?"

"Nina, we've been friends forever. We get angry sometimes, but we're still here for each other. We're as loyal to each other as the Daltonites. However, I do have two questions. Two questions you're probably tired of hearing from me, but I have to ask them again. Is the group worth it? Is Scott worth it?"

"Yes, to both questions. Especially to the

one about Scott. But I really hurt him with one of my lies. If I came within ten feet of him now, he'd set a world-class sprint record going in the opposite direction."

Peggy tried to cheer me up, but it didn't help. At least our friendship wasn't in jeopardy. We'd known each other for a long time. Would anyone else even listen to me? Did I deserve a hearing?

Later that evening I stared at my phone. The vellum invitation for Ginger's party was perched next to the desk lamp. Next to it was a sheet of much-scribbled-on loose-leaf paper. I'd actually written down what I planned to say. I was taking no chance on improvising. I dialed but hung up before finishing the seven digits. I tried again. A second of deadly silence before the connection was made. My fingers burned. *Put the phone back, Nina!*

"Hello? Hello? Is someone there?"

I cleared my throat. "Um, hi, Ginger. It's me, Nina. Nina Ward."

It was her turn to clear her throat. "Oh, hello."

"I suppose you wonder why I'm calling." Wow! Did that sound formal. But it was what the script read. "You have every reason to hang up—"

"I agree."

I realized I wasn't prepared for what Ginger would say. She wouldn't be so easy to approach as Peggy had been. Ginger knew the Nina of the last few months, and my credibility rating was low. Ignoring the carefully planned script, I begged. "Please, I just want to say a few things. Then hang up."

"You want to apologize?" Sarcasm colored her tone.

Maybe I should have hung up and forgotten the whole . . . "Yes, I'm sorry. Truly sorry for lying."

"Your lies didn't hit me directly. I knew you exaggerated about the rock concert. The story got bigger and funnier in the retelling during our trip to the city. But I didn't think anything of it. We all exaggerate once in awhile."

"Once in awhile," I murmured. My grip on the phone loosened.

"You make a career of stories, though. You really hurt Scott. He's practically in shock. He never dreamed you would lie to him. How could you do that?" she demanded.

"I—I didn't mean to. I couldn't tell him the truth—that Rory O'Toole is conceited and egotistical and mean."

"But he found out anyway, in a pretty cruel and embarrassing way."

"I don't know what else to say," I said lamely. "I had a speech written out, one that's the whole truth and nothing but the truth, so help me, but I wrote it with a felt-tipped pen, and every time I blink, tears blur the next line. Not that it matters. I didn't write lines for you. I wrote them for me. To prove to myself I can tell the truth. And for Scott, too, I guess. For the same reason."

Unexpectedly I heard a soft chuckle. "Nina, it's impossible for me to stay angry with you."

"It is?" I clutched the phone again.

"Yeah, but remember, your lies didn't hurt me. They crushed Scott. He always said it was your openness and funny talk that made him fall for you. Now he's found out that it's all been a façade. I don't know if he'll get over it."

"I'd like to apologize to him."

"If you can get near him," Ginger said. "The other kids are sort of protective of him. You can't blame them. Daisy unfortunately told them the Audrey Van modeling show story. She pointed out that just about everything you'd ever said needed closer inspection. They doubt *everything*, Nina, and they're trying to keep Scott from any further hurt." She sighed. "Why'd you do it?"

Her question surprised me. Of course, she wouldn't know. I figured I didn't have anything to lose. I plunged in and told her about my desperate desire to impress the group.

"You're kidding? We're that awesome?" I could almost see her shaking her head from side to side, her blue eyes growing in wonderment. "You know, we're not the only ones, though. You kids from Maitland always avoid us like the plague. You act like we're a bunch of snobs or something. That's one reason we stick together." She was silent for a few seconds. "Well, none of this completely excuses you for some of the things you made up."

I sniffled at her words, and another felt-tipped line smeared. "But it does explain why you lied. Nina, you have to understand, I don't know if Scott will accept an apology—"

I gripped the phone tighter. "It doesn't matter. I just think I should try."

"I agree."

That was the second time she'd uttered those words. This time they encouraged me. "But how? More to the point, where? There's no place in school except for the cafeteria and that's so noi—"

"School is the wrong place. My party is the right place."

"Ginger, I can't come to your party. Facing the kids—"

"You face them in school."

"Not really. Mostly I steer clear and pray no one says anything nasty to me. Look at the awful oral book report I gave. Standing in front of the kids in a controlled environment, I was a basket case. But at a party. They could drown me in the punch bowl, not to mention the Atlantic Ocean."

"You're exaggerating again!" Ginger teased. "Nina, it's a good place. You can get Scott off to the side, and if things don't go well, you know you could hide up in my room. I'll understand even if the others won't. Will you do it?" When I hesitated, she said, "Is Scott important to you?"

"Important and worth it," I replied. "I'll be there."

Chapter Seventeen

My parents were amazed that I wanted to attend the party. I spent hours getting dressed. I chose the green wool dress I'd wanted to wear into the city—on that long ago perfect day—and swept my hair up on top of my head. Even so, I felt totally unpartylike when I stopped in the hallway to get my coat.

But Mom saved the evening. "You look absolutely beautiful!" she said, hugging me. "Everything will be OK."

"It will? Then why do I feel like I'm about to face a firing squad instead of a group of sophomores?" Why had I agreed to this? The kids hadn't been any friendlier after my talk with Ginger. And she had told me at the lockers the next morning that she wouldn't speak up for me. I couldn't blame her. I'd gotten myself into this predicament, and I had to get myself out.

On the radio that morning, I'd heard the Lincoln hockey team had been blown out by the last-place team in our division. Scott must have been devastated. If I'd been with him, I could've cheered him up. With lies? No! My relationship with Scott hadn't been based entirely on lies. Our feelings weren't lies.

Dad drove me to Ginger's. "What time should I pick you up?" he asked as we turned onto the highway.

"Maybe you should stick around. I might dash in and out."

"Your mother filled me in on what's been going on. Now I understand all your questions about my battle with smoking. You wanted to quit telling stories."

"Lies." I leaned my head against the back of the seat. "I was as addicted to them as you were to cigarettes. I wanted to quit cold turkey like you did. Only my chance slipped by."

"You have a second chance, Nina. Otherwise, you wouldn't be sticking your neck out by going to this party."

"Maybe." I remained quiet for the rest of the trip. Mom, Dad, Peggy, Bobby, and Ginger were all so understanding. I didn't deserve it. However, I sensed they were probably the only ones who would be sympathetic. Oh, maybe Wendie or Ace would come around in time. But Daisy, Duane, Marty? Maybe never at all. And Scott? A lost cause? I gripped my purse. Please don't let him be! I prayed. Let me get through to him! I glanced at the brightly wrapped gift on the seat between Dad and me. They were tapes for Ginger's new car. Scott and I had bought them the night before the horrible scene with Rory. "We'll leave them at your house," Scott had said. "You probably wrap things better than I do." He'd never asked about the gift. He'd probably gone out and bought something else for Ginger. A gift from him alone. Shivers went through me. The first of the evening but certainly not the last.

I asked Dad to pick me up at eleven. I'd declined Ginger's invitation to stay over. "If I make a fool of myself again, I want to cry myself to sleep in my own bed," I'd told her yesterday afternoon at the lockers.

Dad pulled into the curved driveway. Several cars already lined it. "Don't go any closer," I said. "Walking up to the door might clear my head."

"Good luck, Nina," Dad said, kissing my forehead. "Your mother and I are proud of you for taking this step. It's a brave one, all things considered."

Dad's words buoyed me. Plus the fact that

no one else was walking along the driveway. I neared the house. I could do it. I could face the Daltonites!

I couldn't face the Daltonites.

A car turned up the driveway, and I hid—I ducked behind a black station wagon. I watched Wendie get out and walk to the door.

Who was I kidding? I'd trembled that day in oral communications when I gave my first speech and had to face all the Daltonites. They didn't even have feelings one way or the other about me then. How could I honestly expect myself to brave them en masse tonight when I knew for sure most of them hated me?

There was a window open slightly, and Daisy's bubbly voice carried over to my hiding place. "I had the best time last night. Just the best! Bobby is darling!"

"I'm glad you enjoyed yourself," Marty said. "Because the game was a bummer."

"What did you expect? Scott couldn't get himself going. He's so down," Wendie said.

"Well, of course. Nina really hurt him," Daisy said acidly. The voices faded as they moved away from the window.

I remained rigid, my boots digging into the snow-covered sandy soil. The icy ocean wind blasted through my wool coat.

They'd never forgive me! And if *they* wouldn't, Scott certainly wouldn't. After all, I'd hurt him more than anyone.

Where was he? Maybe he was coming with Ace. His car wasn't in the drive yet. Or maybe he was already inside. With a date? My thoughts were torturing me! I remembered the hurt in his gray eyes. *I'd* put the hurt there.

I tightened the coat around me. I should've asked my father to stick around. I stared down at the present, then looked at the front door. Quiet strains of a love song reached me. What could I do? The back door! Maybe Mrs. Callison or one of Ginger's brothers would be in the kitchen. I could give them the present, ask them to get Ginger, and beg her to let me stay in her room until eleven when my father was due to pick me up.

I trudged to the rear of the house, music and laughter following me from inside the house. It must be a super party, I thought. I reached the kitchen door and glanced in the window. Two people were inside, but they weren't Mrs. Callison or Ginger's brothers. I froze, staring at Wendie and Daisy, who were getting soft drinks from the refrigerator. I ducked quickly when Wendie whirled around. Had she seen me? Not likely. She said something I couldn't make out. But Daisy's shrill voice carried, as usual. "You must be imagining things! She wouldn't show her face here. C'mon, I don't want to miss a thing at this party!" Wendie must've said something else because Daisy repeated, "Honestly, Wendie! She wouldn't *dare* come. We've made it clear how we feel about the little liar. C'mon!"

Yes, they'd made it perfectly clear! I ran blindly, stumbling to the rear of the Callison property. Tears streamed down my cold cheeks. My mascara burned my eyes. I tripped along, nose running, gift and pocketbook bumping at my sides. Where was I headed? Suddenly I knew. The gazebo. A special place. I dashed into it. It was probably an illusion, but as soon as I entered it, I felt warmer and safer. A brilliant star-filled night provided some light. I wiped off the bench with my gloves and sat down. After finding a tissue and blowing my nose, I sat and cried. My sobbing and the bits of music from the house blocked out all other sounds, which was why I didn't hear the new noise until it was practically upon me. My first thought was that Igor and Ivan were on the loose. I wasn't frightened, just surprised.

The surprise turned into astonishment

when I saw the person who entered the gazebo. We both said, "Oh!" simultaneously.

"I—I had no idea." Scott spoke first.

"I was just sitting here, passing time. Ginger's on her way out here to get her pre—" I did it again! Lied glibly! I shook my head fiercely. "That's an out-and-out lie. I couldn't face anyone, so I ran out here to hide." Could he tell I'd been crying? Had he heard the sobs? He leaned against a pillar, saying nothing.

"Actually, I really wanted to talk to you." I took a deep breath. Icy air filled my lungs, and ridiculously I wondered if that was a way to catch pneumonia. Not caring if it was, I rushed on. "Scott, I've wanted to talk to you all week, but I couldn't get near you."

"Funny, I always figured you could accomplish anything you wanted," he said in a whisper.

"Oh, if I could cushion myself with a good story," I said softly. "But I don't have any stories, any lies, tonight."

Was it my imagination, or was my courage gathered from being here, in this place that was special to both Scott and me? "I wanted to let you know I'm sorry for what happened with Rory. It was all my fault. He never said anything about the Lincoln High team, except when he bragged about his great exploits. He has an ego bigger than Alaska." I paused for an encouraging sound or sign from Scott. Neither was forthcoming. My heart pounded, and I was sure he could hear it in the still night.

"I—I wanted you to believe he was a fan of yours because you admired him so much. I didn't have the heart to tell you he was an egomaniacal idiot. You idolized him. I couldn't bear to tell you the truth."

"So you let me make a fool of myself," he shot out, machine-gun fashion.

His words stung. "I never thought you'd walk over to him and try to strike up a conversation. I was only concerned with telling the right story, not with the consequences. Ha!" I shook my head. "I never believed there'd be any."

He moved but not near me. He was purposely keeping his distance, which was no mean feat considering the size of our quarters. A lump formed in my throat. I'd leave. I'd walk home. Scott's words stopped me before I could stand up.

"Just as it never occurred to me to question anything you said."

"You—you should have. Maybe if you had, maybe if all the others had—"

But Scott wasn't listening. "That first speech you gave in oral communications overwhelmed me. I'd had my eye on you, anyhow, but that speech—I couldn't believe it! Then when you showed an interest in me, I was even more stunned."

I had to interrupt. "You were stunned that *I* was interested in *you*? You're everything—handsome, a star athlete, sensitive—face it, not many boys would find a gazebo romantic. Most boys don't know what a gazebo is."

He chuckled. Just barely, but I heard it. Did I have a chance? I plunged on. "You're also a Daltonite, which carries a lot of weight. And it was the main reason I made up all the lies. I wanted to impress the kids and keep you interested in me. Most of all keep you interested in me."

"I don't get it."

"The kids, you're all so close. I figured if they approved of me, you wouldn't stop seeing me—"

"But I was already crazy about you."

Was. Past tense. Bad sign. Well, I couldn't expect miracles. At least Scott was listening. "I wasn't sure of anything. Not at first. So I kept spinning tales. Then when I became more confident about us, I just couldn't stop the lies. They made me sound wittier, more acceptable to the kids."

A lengthy silence was punctuated by the howling wind, ocean breakers crashing on the shore, and the almost perceptible strains of a Billy Joel song. Scott sat on the edge of the bench.

"I am sorry," I said softly. "I did a very, very dumb thing. A lot of dumb things. I don't expect us to be 'us' anymore, but could you at least say you understand why I acted so stupidly?"

"Nina, I have to explain something." Now that he was closer, I could see the strain on his face. He looked worn out. If I could have looked into a mirror right then, that description would have fit me, too. "I never thought to question you about Rory—"

"Because you trusted me."

"Yeah. But there was more. I was too flattered by what you'd told me. I get pretty full of myself sometimes—"

"You?" I gasped.

"You'd better believe it. A big-time hockey player, a beautiful girlfriend, and the legendary Rory O'Toole thinking I was terrific."

"You are," I murmured.

He shrugged. "If I was so terrific, I should've noticed that your stories—"

"Lies."

"OK, lies. That your lies were a bit out of hand. Nina, I knew the Parkhurst team didn't have a game the night of your party."

"They didn't? I thought they always played on Saturday night. Wait a minute, you knew I'd lied about Rory playing that night and didn't say anything to me?"

"Not exactly," he admitted. "I figured one of two ways. One, he'd told you they had a game in order to get out of coming to the party, or two, he'd declined, and you were trying to spare my feelings."

"I was. But I went about it in the wrong way."

"Well, I should have said something. We're some pair!"

"Are we a pair?" I whispered.

He moved closer. My heart thumped faster. He brushed back a loose tendril of my hair. "Do you see any of the other couples sitting out here, freezing and crying?" His eyes were misty! "In a romantic gazebo? Nina, I came out here because I was drawn to it. Do you know what I mean?"

I nodded. He touched my chin. Our glances locked. His large hands held my small ones. "We could be a pair. We'd have to work at it.

Things were good for us, and it wasn't all an illusion."

"Not at all," I said, feeling warmth on my face.

"No more little white lies?"

"None."

Scott kissed me deeply. I trembled and, after the long kiss, rested my head on his shoulder. Although being in his arms made me all toasty, I suddenly cared very, very much about getting pneumonia sitting in this wonderfully romantic but icy gazebo. I had too many things to do, one of which was to face the Daltonites. After facing myself, maybe that wouldn't be so difficult. I took Scott's hand, and we walked to the Callison house.

Sweet
Dreams